DRAEKON MATE

EXILED TO THE PRISON PLANET

LEE SAVINO
LILI ZANDER

D1521758

*Thanks to Miranda and Sandy Ebel, beta-readers extraordinaire.
You make our stories better.*

Cover Design by Kasmit Covers

DRAEKON MATE

Crashed spaceship. Prison planet. Snarling, lethal predators. Two big, hulking, bronzed aliens who turn into dragons.

The best part? The dragons insist I'm their mate.

The Zorahn wanted women for some kind of super-secret science experiment, and I volunteered. *Dumb move, right?* But they promised we'd be safe, and they offered a lot of money. *Money I needed desperately.*

Of course, everything went wrong.

Our spaceship has crashed on a prison planet, one where the Zorahn exile their most dangerous criminals. My friends are injured. I'm all alone on a jungle planet where everything is designed to kill me.

Then I run into the Draekons. When they see me, they change into dragons and burn the predators threatening me to a crisp. They feed me and care for me, and they keep me safe.

But there's a catch. The Draekons insist that I'm their mate. And the only way they can shift into dragons again to save my friends? *Both of them need to mate with me. At the same time.*

This isn't the space vacation I thought it would be.

Draekon Mate is the first book in the new Dragons in Exile series. It's a full-length, standalone science fiction dragon-shifter MFM menage romance story featuring a snarky human female, and two arrogant aliens that keep her warm, with or without dragon fire. (No M/M) Happily-ever-after guaranteed!

ARE YOU ALL CAUGHT UP WITH THE DRAEKONS?

DRAGONS IN EXILE

DRAEKON DESIRE - Binge-read the entire **DRAGONS IN EXILE** series in one heavily discounted, 1000+ page boxed set!

Or read the individual books:
Draekon Mate - Viola's story

Draekon Fire - Harper's story
Draekon Heart - Ryanna's story
Draekon Abduction - Olivia's story
Draekon Destiny - Felicity's story
Daughter of Draekons - Harper's birth story
Draekon Fever - Sofia's story
Draekon Rogue - Bryce's story
Draekon Holiday - A holiday story

REBEL FORCE
Draekon Warrior - Alice & Kadir
Draekon Conquerer - Lani & Ruhan
Draekon Pirate - Diana & Mirak
Draekon Warlord - Naomi & Danek
Draekon Guardian - Liz & Sixth - coming soon!

*The **Must Love Draekons** newsletter is your source for all things Draekon. Subscribe today and receive a free copy of Draekon Rescue, a special Draekon story not available for sale.*

THE LOWLANDS AND SURROUNDING AREAS

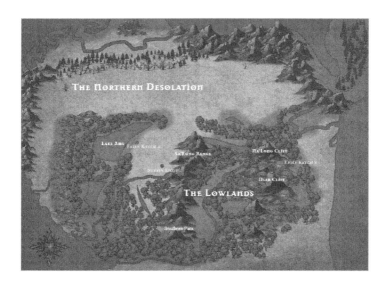

1

VIOLA

I thought it'd be bigger.

This is the first thought I have when I enter the gleaming golden spaceship of the Zorahn.

That's what she said. I hide my grin at my stupid little joke. I always joke when I'm nervous, and it turns out stepping onto an alien craft to be carried off to a planet several light years away is about a thousand times more nerve-wracking than giving a dissertation to a panel of world-renowned botanists. *About several thousand times more nerve-wracking.*

It took countless pep talks from my dad and a slug of whiskey to get me over that last hurdle to my Ph.D. It's going to take a few bottles to get me comfortable on this alien ship. The Zorahn craft isn't even as large as a commercial airliner. It's ten feet across, and forty feet long, and the insides gleam with the same golden hue as the exterior. Even more worryingly, there are no seats to be seen.

This is not going to be a comfortable trip.

Then the reality sinks in. There is life out there in the universe—we are not alone. Aliens exist. I'm on a real, live spaceship, heading to the planet of Zoraht, home of the Zorahn. I won't see Earth again for six months.

I look around, and the faces of the women next to me all betray the same emotions. Awe. Fear. Excitement. Up until a few weeks ago, we were just civilians going about our normal daily life.

Now we're astronauts. *Insane.*

Major Schultz, the US Army officer who's been functioning as a liaison between the Zorahn and us, clears his throat for attention. "As you know," he begins, "this is a momentous day for humanity."

The woman next to me, a tall, lean blonde, rolls her eyes. "God, he likes to hear himself talk," she mutters under her breath. Her name is Harper, I remember, from the team-building exercises the Army made us participate in once we'd been chosen by the Zorahn. She's a swim coach in California who almost made the national team in college.

Hector Schultz either doesn't hear her or pretends not to. "The ten of you," he says, "have been chosen by our honored guests, the Zorahn, to travel to their planet and discover the wonders of their world."

The way Hector Schultz makes it sound, we're space tourists. That's not even close to the truth.

The real reason we're on this ship? Our genes. According to the emissaries, Zoraht, the homeworld of the Zorahn, is being ravaged by a mysterious disease, and their scientists need our genetic material to devise a cure.

We're glorified lab rats.

"Remember that the thoughts of every single human on planet Earth are with you," he continues solemnly. "You represent the first step in an alliance that we hope will span generations."

He looks like he could go on for hours, but one of the

Zorahn males clears his throat, and Hector Schultz takes the hint. His voice trails off, and he stands in the middle of the ship, looking uncomfortable and out of place.

The Zorahn male who interrupted Schultz' monologue steps forward. He's seven feet tall. His skin is bronzed, his head is clean-shaven, and his body is hard and corded with muscle. Blue tattooed whorls cover his bald head, though the rest of his body is unmarked. I think his name is Beirax. He wears black pants, but in place of a shirt, intricate bands of blue fabric cover his chest.

He's intimidating as fuck.

He says something, the words harsh and garbled in my ears. I have no idea what he's saying, and I turn to look at Harper, wondering if she can understand him any better than me. The tall blonde is frowning, her arms crossed over her chest.

Nope. Not just me. The only one who seems to have any clue what the Zorahn said is Schultz.

Noticing our looks of confusion, Beirax snaps a question to the other male on board the ship, Mannix. Mannix is just as tall as his fellow alien, but his tattoos are black and brown, not blue. I'm sure the coloring has some significance, though what it is we don't know. The Zorahn haven't bothered to tell us much about their culture. All we know is that the High Emperor rules the entire planet and we will be under his personal protection when we are on Zoraht.

Mannix shakes his head. He holds his palm over a wall panel, and it slides open, revealing a storage cavity packed with mysterious and unidentifiable objects. Pulling a handful of small golden disks out, he hands one to each of us, and mimes that we're to insert the disks in our right ear.

Ah. Translator. That's why Schultz didn't look as confused as the rest of us.

Harper snorts. "No need for the lab rats to understand what they're saying," she says dryly. She lifts the button-sized device to her ear. I do the same, yelping as a spark runs through me at the point of contact.

"No kidding," I mutter, rubbing at my ear. "Also, no need to tell us that the damn thing should come with a warning label. I guess they don't have lawyers on Zoraht."

"We don't." Beirax's voice drips with frost. "If you could return your attention to me, Viola Lewis?"

Ahem. The translator's working then. Good to know that the first alien sentence I hear is a scolding.

A couple of the women giggle, but they stop as soon as they feel the full force of the Zorahn's glare. "As I was saying," he continues, "You are passengers on *Fehrat 1*. The journey to the homeworld will take ten of your Earth days. You will be placed in stasis for the trip. Any questions?"

Multiple hands fly in the air. Beirax sighs in frustration and points to a petite dark-haired woman. "Sofia Menendez," he intones. "Yes?"

I wonder if the Zorahn understand the concept of a first and last name. The way Beirax refers to us, I doubt it. Viola Lewis. Sofia Menendez. Either that or he has a stick up his butt.

The last of the Zorahn, Raiht'vi, chooses this moment to enter the spaceship. She's a lot taller than most human women, but her build is similar to ours. She has a narrow waist and wider hips, and her clothing, bulky as it is, doesn't hide the swell of her breasts.

As tall as the men, she's the only one with hair on her head. The scarlet tresses are tightly braided and decorated with objects that look like shells, and her clothing is white. "Are we ready to leave, Beirax?" she asks, a forbidding expression on her face.

"The humans have questions, Highborn," Beirax says apologetically. "According to the orders of the High Emperor..."

She cuts him off. "I'm aware of Lenox's commands." She gives us an unsmiling look. "Satisfy their curiosity. We leave in a knur."

One Knur equals Twelve Earth Minutes, the device in my ear helpfully interjects.

Twelve minutes until we're off planet. I take a deep breath and wipe my sweaty palms on my NASA-issued clothing, made from a navy material that fits like a second skin. The last few weeks of training and a highly nutritious diet have left me fitter than I've ever been in my life, but I still don't care for the government-issued Spandex. "Why can't we wear normal clothing?" I'd asked when a grim-faced captain handed them to me.

"The suits are specially formulated for space travel. The nanotechnology cleans itself and will help regulate your body temperature."

"Does it come in pink?" When he didn't crack a smile at the wisecrack, I'd mumbled, "Navy isn't really my color."

"You are a representative of the United States," he'd replied tersely. "You will dress the part."

So I stand in the Zorahn ship with the other women, the ten of us looking like an Olympic ski team. If the aliens think it's weird that we're dressed identically, they don't say anything.

Raiht'vi, the female Zorahn, disappears into the cockpit of the spaceship. At least, that's what I think it is, given the number of instrument panels on the dashboard. It's also the only part of the ship that has a window.

Look at the blue skies, Viola. You won't see them again for six months.

Sofia, who is fresh out of medical residency, asks her question. "The translator is speaking English to me," she says. "I'm bilingual. How did it decide what language to use?"

Her question seems to puzzle Beirax and Mannix. "The translator doesn't decide," Beirax replies, a confused expression on his face. "The translator *translates*."

"Why didn't it translate to Spanish?" Sofia persists.

Beirax frowns. "The translator translates Zor to English and vice-versa. That is its purpose."

Not a universal translator then. That shit probably only exists in the imaginations of sci-fi writers.

"Excuse me?" A soft voice at my elbow makes me turn. A stunning redhead with a perfect figure and flawless pale skin stands at my side, biting her lower lip. I blink, and even the alien falls silent.

"Hi, I'm Olivia," she says, with a little wave of a manicured hand. "I can't get my translator to work." She holds the device up and shakes it, all the while wearing an adorable little pout.

If I were going to set up an intergalactic dating service, I'd definitely put bombshell Olivia Buckner's picture front and center.

"Try sticking it in your ear," Harper quips. She and I exchange glances as Mannix gets another translator, and Schultz about falls over himself to help her put it in. Even Beirax can't take his eyes off her gravity-defying breasts. Male interest in a hot female is universal.

My gaze drifts over the muscles of the brown tattooed alien, Mannix. Are Zorahn cocks like human males?

Focus, Vi!

After much attention from the men, Olivia finally has her translator installed, and Beirax signals he's ready for the next question. A woman with short curly brown hair raises her hand like she's in grade school. "You said stasis," she says nervously. "Is that safe?"

"Of course it is." Schultz rushes to reply before either of the Zorahn can answer. He looks indignant. "Everything on this ship has been tested. The United States government is deeply invested in your safety and well-being."

Mannix gives Schultz an irritated look at the interruption. "The High Emperor has decreed your safety. It is so."

"This High Emperor must be quite the guy," Harper Boyd murmurs.

I don't doubt it. As a gesture of good faith, the Zorahn came bearing gifts. One of them was the cure for leukemia. Rumor has it that lung cancer is next on the list, and the tobacco companies are practically drooling at the prospect of being able to market their wares again without health concerns.

I don't know what else the Zorahn promised our government to get them to sanction shooting us into space, but whatever they offered, it's gotta be huge. Much bigger than cancer. Once the Zorahn told them what they wanted, the government fell over itself to cooperate with the aliens. They even got the media in lockstep. I've seen article after article gush about the Zorahn, calling them our allies, even our saviors.

The way I see it, the Zorahn spaceship could be a tin can, and I doubt the government would care. There's too much superior alien technology at stake.

May Archer looks worried, biting her lip. I nudge her. "I'm sure we'll be fine," I say, keeping my tone reassuring. "The Zorahn want us to arrive safely as much as we do." We've been told our genes could save their race, but only if they can study us in their high-tech space-age labs. Thus the journey to their planet.

Beirax makes a chopping gesture with his hand. "No more questions," he says tersely. "Hector Schultz, it is time for you to leave. We depart for Zoraht in a pars."

One pars equals Six Earth Minutes, my translator chirps.

Six minutes to go. I glance around at the nine other women, but no one in our little space sorority seems excited anymore. Reality has set in.

Who volunteers to leave Earth behind and travel to an alien planet for six months? What kind of person chooses to trust the emissaries when they promise our safe return, guaranteed by the High Emperor of Zoraht himself? Why would anyone line up to be poked and prodded by alien scientists?

The answers are simple. Money. Adventure. And in my case, a lack of anything left on Earth to live for.

Schultz salutes us briskly and departs, clattering down the ramp. There are no windows on the sides of the ship, so I can't see the crowds outside. Maybe some of the other women have family watching them depart. Not me. I have no family left. My mother left when I was ten, and my father died of leukemia two months before the cure came. Yeah, I know. *Irony.*

I watch as Beirax and Mannix hold their palms over several large panels in the back, which slide open to reveal the stasis pods. Ever seen a picture of the capsule hotels in Japan? That's what these resemble. "Are we going to be awake during the trip?" I blurt out without thinking.

This time, Beirax actually rolls his eyes. "It is a stasis pod, Viola Lewis. By definition..." His voice trails off, and he sneers at me.

Yeah. I'm making a great first impression.

I AWAKEN with a lurch and bang my head against the ceiling of my stasis pod. "Ouch," I groan, rubbing at the spot. Pain wars with excitement and excitement wins.

We must be landing on Zoraht.

The panel opens, and I peer out eagerly. I'm here. I'm on a different planet, halfway across the galaxy. I'm going to see an alien world.

Then I realize that something's wrong. The three Zorahn are standing in the center of the craft, and one of them, Beirax, has a weapon pointed at the other two. "I'm sorry, Highborn," he's saying. "I have other plans for the humans."

"Lenox guaranteed their safety." The female Zorahn, Raiht'vi, speaks through clenched teeth. " You've altered the ship's course and locked the controls. What are you doing? This is treason."

"No." Beirax's voice is eerily calm, and his hand, the one holding the alien gun, is steady. "I commit no treason. I answer to a higher authority."

"Traitor." Raiht'vi looks ready to tear Beirax apart from limb to limb with her bare fingers. "There is no higher authority than Lenox." She glances at the cockpit and sees something on the screen that causes her to gasp out. "No," she whispers. "That is the prison planet. You cannot mean..." Her eyes go wild, and her voice rises in pitch. "What are you doing, Beirax? No ship can survive the asteroid belt. We will all die!"

Asteroid belt? Prison planet? *What the hell?*

Goosebumps rise on my skin. Something very bad is going on—bad enough that Raiht'vi thinks we're all going to die, and Mannix looks like he's going to wet himself—and my instincts warn me not to get in the middle of it. I don't want to know how effective the Zorahn weapon can be.

Over the whine of the engines, I think I hear the other women stir in their stasis pods. *Don't move, don't move,* I beg. *Don't do anything to draw attention to yourselves.*

Beirax draws himself to his full height. "For a thousand years," he intones, "we have sinned against the Draekons. We have used them and imprisoned them. We have exiled them to a harsh and hostile world." His eyes glow with an inner fire. "And we, the Order of the Crimson Night, have sworn never to forget."

Sinned. Imprisoned. Exiled. Whatever Beirax is talking about, it isn't giving me the warm and fuzzies. Who are the Draekons, and what the hell kind of fucked up politics have we landed in the middle of?

The ship lurches. As I watch, my heart pounding in my throat, its trajectory changes. A red planet looms in the view screen, and the nose of the ship tilts inexorably toward it.

We start to descend.

Scratch that. Descend suggests that we're landing with a measure of control. From the panic etched on Raiht'vi's face, from the way my stomach's churning, I don't think we're landing.

We're crashing.

"The Draekons will rip us apart, Beirax." Raiht'vi tries again, one last desperate appeal. "You fool, don't you understand? Even if we survive the landing, they will destroy us. You must let me correct our course before it's too late."

Beirax remains unmoved. "I chose exile and even death so the Draekons may rise again." His voice rises to a chant. "It is foretold. The humans were the seed that gave life to the Draekon. And I, Beirax, will provide the seed anew. The human women will restore the Draekons to the glory that is their birthright."

Part of me struggles to understand what's going on. The other part of me is frozen in horror. We're going to crash on an alien world. One that's reduced Mannix to a blubbering mess, one that's caused Raiht'vi's face to whiten with terror.

The hum of the engines grows louder. We're definitely falling now. Asteroids hammer at the body of the ship from every direction. I cling onto the ridged walls of my stasis pod, trying to hold on. I don't know if the others are awake. All I can do is hope that they're safe.

With a dreadful screech, the right wing breaks off. I see it on the viewscreen, the metal hurtling away from us. The ship immediately rolls into a spiral. Panels spring open, their contents erupting into the main area.

It is chaos.

The ship gets hotter, and it becomes difficult to breathe. My stomach is churning. A sudden reel of the ship has me flying through the air, tumbling toward the walls.

Then I collide against a hard surface with a sickening thud, and everything goes dark.

ARAX

"I dreamed about you last night," I tell Nyx as the two of us jog through the plains, pursuing a herd of *argangana*. The swift-footed beasts are difficult to catch, but they're our main source of meat in this world. The rainy season is almost on us—yesterday, the green moon Uzzan had barely been visible in the night sky—and we need to stock up on food ahead of the torrential downpours that flood the lowlands and make hunting impossible.

"Should I be flattered?" Nyx's lips curve into a sly grin. "Has the lack of women in this world finally changed your preferences, Firstborn?"

I laugh despite myself. On Zoraht, Nyx's words would be treasonous, but one of the things I like the most about the dark-haired man is his complete lack of reverence. Some of the other exiles still cling to the rigid social structures of Zoraht. Not Nyx.

"It wasn't that sort of dream." My smile fades as the memories come to the forefront.

Lines of young men await the Testing; I'm one of them. Nyx is in line, too, his sleeve rolled up, showing the nineteen tattoos on his forearm.

"We were in the main market area of Vissa, you and I. It was the time of the Testing."

"Ah." Nyx's face turns sober. None of us like to remember the day we tested positive for the Draekon mutation. "I wasn't tested in Vissa. My Testing was in Giflan."

Giflan, the city by the sea, with its purple cliffs and soft blue skies. We had a home there. I remember running along the interior corridors, weaving through the throngs of people, Lenox at my heels, the guards panting behind us as they struggled to catch up with their young royal charges.

"Mine was in the Royal Palace," I reply. "But in my dream, we were side by side in the market tents."

The indigo-clad Scientist holds the golden-tipped needle of the Draekon tester against my flesh and pierces my skin. Nineteen times, the tester has flashed green. This time, it flashes crimson.

"Do you know what it does?"

The *argangana* are tiring. The herd's pace slows, and we are close to catching up with them. I reach for my throwing knives. At my side, Nyx does the same. "What?"

"The Draekon mutation," Nyx replies. "Do you know what it does? There are rumors, but the truth is sealed for most citizens."

Our footsteps slow as we near the herd. We will need to bring down six of the beasts so we have enough to eat during the rainy season. Nyx and I have outpaced the other hunters, but Rorix and Ferix are at our heels, as are Vulrux and Thrax.

"The prevailing theory in the back streets of Vissa," Nyx continues, "is that the Draekon mutation is a plot hatched by the Highborn and the scientists to keep the populace afraid and obedient." He shoots me a sidelong look. "Until I saw you on the Exile ship, I would have said the same thing."

Until he saw the Firstborn of Zoraht, exiled along with the others. The Draekon mutation does not care for the blood status of its victims. Highborn or Lowborn, no one is immune.

Nyx is watching me carefully, waiting for my reply.

According to the sealed records of the ThoughtVaults, twelve hundred years ago, the scientists created a race of soldiers called Draekons who could turn into beasts at will. These beast-men conquered the stars and expanded the Zoraht Empire, but over time, they rebelled against their masters and sought freedom from a life of war.

Terrified at the thought of their creations running amok, the Zorahn scientists sought to kill the Draekons, but they were only partially successful. They couldn't completely wipe out the Draekon gene. It manifests itself in the general population and seems resistant to eradication.

Since the scientists can't destroy it, they've opted for the next best thing. They round up anyone who possesses the Draekon mutation, and they exile them on a prison planet.

Do I believe I'm going to transform into a beast? *No, of course not.* Yet, it is the reason for our exile on this prison planet. For sixty seasons, we've been cut off from our families and our home. For sixty seasons, we've languished in this jungle world. Here we will remain for the rest of our lives. There is no hope of rescue—no Zorahn pilot possesses the reflexes required to navigate the asteroid belt surrounding this planet without wrecking their ship.

Our lives are simple. Hunt and gather food in the lowlands during the dry season. Retreat to the high cliffs when the rains come. Survive.

Draekon mutation or not, this is now our home.

The silence stretches. "What does it matter?" I say finally, my tone dismissive. "Here we are, and here we will remain." Spotting my target, I throw my knives with both hands. Two *argangana* fall.

Nyx brings down two more without speaking. The rest of the herd stampedes.

We stride forward to retrieve our knives and are about to set off in pursuit of the herd once more when Nyx grabs my shoulder. "Arax," he says, pointing upward, the tone of his voice urgent. "What's that?"

I look up. Something is dropping from the sky, the air aflame around it. As we watch, it falls faster and then it goes out of view, hidden behind the Na'Lung cliffs.

My heart starts to race.

We've been on this planet for sixty seasons; we've never seen anything like it. "Is it another exile batch?" Nyx wonders out loud.

I shake my head. "Unlikely." Though we've been here for years, we have yet to see any other signs of habitation. "The scientists are not fools. They will not drop another exile batch so close to us."

Could that object in the sky be a ship? Could it be a ticket out of this planet? I must know.

"It's a day's journey to the far side of the Na'Lung cliffs," Nyx says. "I'm assuming we're going to investigate?"

The sun is setting. We have only enough time to mark our kills so that the others can find them, and seek shelter for the night. The lowland jungle is no place to linger after dark; it's too dangerous.

"Yes," I reply. "We leave at first light."

3

VIOLA

Someone is screaming.

I open my eyes slowly. Everything hurts. When I reach up to touch my forehead, it comes away wet with blood.

"Where am I?" I murmur, trying to remember, then everything comes rushing back to me. The argument between Beirax and Raiht'vi. The ship crashing on something called the Prison Planet.

"That's a good question, Viola." Harper's face looms over mine. "Are you okay?"

Not even a little bit. "I think so." I try to sit up, and a wave of dizziness overtakes me. "How long have I been out?"

Harper grimaces, dabbing at my cut with a piece of white cloth. It's a pillowcase from one of the stasis chambers. "As best as I can tell, two hours." She sounds strained and her hand, as she reaches to help me, trembles.

The fog in my head clears a little. "Is everyone fine?"

"Janet's dead," she replies, her eyes filling with tears. "One of the Zorahn men is as well."

"Shit." I must be numb with shock because I feel

nothing more than a twinge for poor Janet, who had been so concerned about the safety of the stasis pods. "Which Zorahn? Beirax or Mannix?"

"I'm not good at names," she replies. "The one with brown tattoos."

"Mannix." I get up, ignoring the way the room swims around me. I can be sick later. "Who's screaming?"

"Olivia. She's broken her leg." She shudders. "We tried to set it, but it's a bad break. The bone is sticking out. Sofia's trying to staunch the bleeding. Paige, Felicity, and Bryce are still in stasis, and I don't want to open the chambers to find out if they're okay."

I grab her shoulder to steady myself and take stock. It's not a pretty picture. We're in the main passenger area. There's a giant hole in the body of the ship, where the wing tore away.The ship must have come to rest on its side because the hole is above my head.

"The air must be breathable," Harper says quietly. "Otherwise we'd all be dead."

I hope for all our sakes that she's right because there's no way to make this ship airtight. Ignoring the outside for the moment, I transfer my attention back to the ship and immediately wish I hadn't. Janet's body is crumpled against one wall, a huge metal spike sticking out of her belly, blood drying all around her, the smell tangy and metallic.

I hastily turn away from her before I lose the contents of my stomach, but the next sight isn't prettier. Olivia's lying on the floor, writhing in pain, and when I see the white bone, my belly churns again.

Ryanna's leaning against the other wall, holding a wad of cloth against her forehead. May's sitting next to her, her right arm hanging limply at her side. "I hit the wall pretty hard," she says when she notices me staring. "And Ryanna cut herself." She gives me another look. "You're bleeding again."

"It's just a flesh wound," I reply automatically, dabbing the cut again with the pillowcase, my eyes continuing to scan the room. Harper's moved back next to Sofia, and the two women are trying to comfort Olivia. I turn my attention away from the weeping redhead and set off in search of the three Zorahn.

I find them in the cockpit. Mannix's body is twisted at an odd and unnatural angle. Harper's right; he's dead.

Raiht'vi's eyes are closed, and her breathing is labored. Beirax, the cause of all this turmoil, is in even worse shape. His entire torso is torn open, and bright blue blood is everywhere. A hysterical sob wells up in my throat when I register the color of his blood, and my knees start to shake. Alien blood is blue. Who knew?

"Viola." Harper hears the wild giggle that escapes my lips, and she's instantly at my side, her hands around my shoulders. "You're in shock. Pull yourself together."

I shake my head to clear it, and the room spins around me. Dumb move. *Don't do that again, Vi.*

Beirax moans in pain and that sound spurs me to action. "We need a plan," I say out loud.

"No shit, Sherlock. Any ideas?"

What would happen on Earth if a ship crash-landed? It would disappear from radar, and the alarm would be sounded almost immediately. I can only hope that space travel is the same way, and the Zorahn know we've crashed. If they do, how long will it take to send a rescue mission?

I make my way back to the main area. "Anyone know what day it is?" I ask the women there. "On Earth, that is."

Ryanna looks up. "There was a timer in my stasis pod," she replies. "It was counting down from ten days."

"There was?" It's a good thing I decided to be a botanist, not a detective. I'd barely even noticed that there was a thin mattress pad and a pillow before I'd gone under. I go to check, and sure enough, Ryanna's right. There is a count-down of some kind, and it's showing that there are still four days to go.

Wherever we crashed, we're only four days away from Zoraht.

Help could be coming for us in less than a week.

Hope trickles through me. One week. We just need to survive on this unknown planet for a week, and then it'll be over. The Zorahn will find us; I'm certain they will. As the emissaries kept telling us, we're under the personal protec-tion of the High Emperor himself. That's gotta count for something, right?

Olivia's cries have died down. Sofia's sitting on the floor next to her, looking drained. "She's out." She nods in the direction of her small doctor's bag. She'd insisted on bringing it with her, and God, I'm glad she did. "I gave her something for the pain, but the relief is only temporary."

"You did good," I say encouragingly. "Help is going to get here in a few days. All we need to do is manage until then. *We're going to be okay.*"

The women look up, their faces hopeful, and I feel like there's a giant spotlight on me. "Here's what I know," I tell them. "Beirax and Raiht'vi were arguing. Beirax pulled a gun on her, and deliberately crashed the ship on this planet."

Their faces show their shock.

"But," I add reassuringly, "The Zorahn have all kinds of advanced technology. They'll find us. Until then, here's the plan. We need to get the injured people into the stasis pods. That's our best shot at keeping them alive."

Sofia looks relieved at my words. "That's a good idea," she says. "Beirax's injuries especially…" Her voice trails off, and she shudders. "I don't have the slightest idea what to do. I don't know anything about Zorahn anatomy."

None of us do. While the Zorahn showed up knowing everything about us, we know startlingly little about them. Until I saw Beirax's blood, it didn't even occur to me that it would be a different color.

May pats Sofia on the back with her good arm.

"The rest of us," I continue, "can do one of two things. We can get back into the pods and wait to be rescued, or we can try to find food and water on this planet."

Harper's lips twist into a grimace. "We can't all go back into the pods, Vi," she points out quietly. "They can only be shut from the outside. One of us will need to be awake."

I wanted adventure? Well, here it is. Bright, shiny, and scary as hell.

Ryanna shakes her head. "No way," she says flatly. "Before anyone gets any stupid ideas, we're not going to leave one of us out here alone, while the rest of us crawl into the safety of the pods. And Viola, don't even think about volunteering."

I close my mouth, and she continues. "We put the injured in stasis, and the four of us," she points to Harper, Sofia, and me, "all go find food and water. Okay?"

"I'm not badly hurt," May protests. "I want to come with you."

Sofia shakes her head immediately. "No," she says firmly. "We have no idea what kind of terrain we're going to run into. We don't know if the planet has any predators. Your forearm is broken. We won't be able to protect you."

Predators. Crap. Never thought about that, and it's not a cheery thought.

"There's something else." I try to remember Raiht'vi's words before he crashed the ship, but the pounding in my head increases. "I overheard the Zorahn talk. I think they exiled some people to this planet? The Draekons, Raiht'vi called them. She was terrified that they were going to tear us all to shreds."

"Well, that's reassuring." Ryanna chews on her lip nervously. Sofia goes pale, and even Harper looks alarmed.

I didn't mean to freak them out, but I can't, in good conscience, keep what I heard from them. On an alien planet, knowledge of the dangers out there could be the difference between life and death.

Salvage this situation, Vi. "We can't do anything until the morning anyway," I say firmly. "Let's get the wounded into the stasis pods, and get some rest. Tomorrow's going to be an eventful day."

It's a lot easier said than done to move the injured into the stasis pods. Raiht'vi's eyes fly open when we try to move her, and she grabs me by the throat. Injured or not, she's really strong. "We are on the prison planet," she hisses. "The Draekons are here. Caeron preserve us all."

I struggle to breathe. Spots swim in front of me. "The Draekons?" I choke out.

Harper and Ryanna grab Raiht'vi's hand, trying to get her to release me. Raiht'vi pays them no attention. Her eyes lock onto me, as focused as a laser. "Men that can take the shape of a beast. You must beware. The Draekons are dangerous. Not to be trusted." Her grip finally slackens, and her hand falls away. I drop to the floor, and Sofia hurries up to me. "I'm okay," I tell her, waving away the petite doctor. "It's all good."

I'm lying; it's not good. Raiht'vi hadn't flinched when

Beirax held a gun to her. She hadn't panicked when we were crashing. But these Draekons, whoever they are, terrify her.

What have we gotten ourselves into?

"She's fainted," Sofia announces, bending over the alien woman. "She doesn't look good. We need to get her into the stasis unit."

It takes effort, but we manage it. Beirax is a lot harder. The male alien is built like a truck. It takes all four of us— Harper, Ryanna, Sofia, and me—to move him. By the time we're done, sweat pours off our faces, and Beirax's dripping bright blue blood everywhere. "I don't know what to do," Sofia whispers, her face pinched with tension as she looks at the injured Zorahn. "I swore an oath..."

"You said it yourself. He's not human." My voice comes out too harsh in the quiet, and I soften my tone before I continue. "You don't know anything about his injuries. You can't do anything for him."

"I know." She's silent for a long time, then she closes her eyes and whispers a prayer. "Santa María, Madre de Dios, ruega por nosotros pecadores, ahora y en la hora de nuestra muerte. Amén."

Unable to translate, my earpiece says solemnly.

I don't need the translator to understand the prayer. My college roommate at the University of Wisconsin was Latina and devoutly Catholic. This prayer is etched in the pathways of my brain.

> Holy Mary, mother of God,
> Pray for us sinners,
> Now and at the hour of our death.
> Amen.

IT TAKES us a few hours in the morning to set out.

First, we drag the mattresses from the unused stasis pods and try to cover up the gaping hole in the ship. Then we figure out how the stasis pods operate by punching every button in sight and using May as our test subject.

Before we leave, we ransack the ship for anything useful. I find a bag and stuff three spare translators inside. Ryanna does the same. Sofia takes her medical bag, though I hope we don't run into an occasion where we need to use it. I grab Beirax's weapon from the cockpit as well, even though I have no idea how to use the horseshoe-shaped object.

I know that I'm on a different world, but it only sinks in when we step outside. We appear to have landed in the middle of an alien jungle. There's a cluster of tall, green-and-black striped reeds to my right. Each reed is fifteen feet tall and ends in a glowing blue orb. Some kind of fruit, I wonder, and the botanist in me itches to explore further.

Harper's staring at the sky, which is a pale crimson in color. Two moons loom on the horizon, one large and green, and the other smaller and blue, with rings around it. The only thing this planet has in common with Earth is the sun, which is bright and yellow, just like ours. She looks as overwhelmed as I feel. "Toto," she says slowly, "we aren't in Kansas anymore."

The air is hot and humid. Last night, the spacesuit did a good job of wicking away moisture, but it was built for space, not a tropical alien planet. The humidity seems to have overloaded the nanothingies, and patches of the fabric are now damp.

I slowly turn in a full circle where I stand, trying to decide which way to go. We're looking for food and water, and we need to avoid the Draekons.

One week. You just have to survive a week in this place.

"The mountain." I point the direction of a tall pillar-like rock formation that juts out into the sky. "If we reach the top, we'll be able to see for miles."

No one has a better idea, so we set off in the direction of the big rock, which resembles a massive cock. On a different day, I'd have giggled about that. Today, we walk in silence in single file. I lead the way, clutching Beirax's weapon with tight fingers, and Harper brings up the rear.

It's hard going. We're walking through a jungle. Pink tree trunks hem us in from every side. The forest floor is covered with a tight carpet of some kind of crunchy grass that breaks when we walk on it. Bushes with neon yellow leaves and bright purple thorns block our path, and we have to detour around them.

"This place looks like Candyland," Harper says, reaching for one of the yellow leaves.

"Or Willy Wonka's Chocolate Factory," I say, grabbing her hand to stop her. "Try not to touch anything. We don't know what's poisonous."

"Right. Good thinking. Thanks." She puts a hand to her head. "The sun is making me woozy."

"It's hot as hell," I agree. "But I'm thinking there has to be a lake or a river somewhere. I mean, look at all this vege-tation." I wave a hand at the lush forest. "Even alien plants need water to grow."

"Let's hope you're right," Harper says.

The women all look wilted and gloomy. This won't do. We need to keep our spirits up. "If we don't find a water source," I tell them, "we can risk eating some of the vegeta-tion, and try to get water that way."

"Thanks, Vi," Ryanna says, her face brightening. I hope I'm not spreading false cheer because one thing is crystal clear. If we can't find a drinking source soon, we won't survive.

WE WALK FOR THREE HOURS, growing thirstier and thirstier with each step we take. "Do you think any of these plants are edible?" Ryanna asks as we pass through a grove of giant trees with pink bark.

"Ask Viola, she's the botanist," Sofia puffs, a little out of breath.

"Yeah, on Earth." I shake my head. "I'm afraid I didn't take 'Alien Flora 101' in school." Mainly because, up until six months ago, we thought that aliens didn't exist.

"When we get back to Earth, you can teach it," Ryanna says.

"Someone's a positive thinker," Harper snickers.

"I just don't want to waste energy on dwelling on all the stuff that can go wrong," Ryanna snaps back.

"Okay, enough. No fighting," I announce, thinking of my dad and what he would say in this situation. "We need to have each other's backs. Together, we can survive."

Harper golf claps. "Ladies, I give you Viola Lewis," she says. "Interplanetary motivational speaker." She smiles to counteract the sarcasm.

"Whatever," I tell Harper. We have enough problems; we don't need to bicker. "I think Ryanna's right. We're hurt, tired, and hungry, and we've crashed on an alien planet. What else can go wrong?"

Famous last words.

Harper trips. Sofia gasps instinctively, but the blonde woman breaks her fall by grabbing the pink tree. Her hand lands dead center on an orange mold that's growing on the bark.

I really wish I hadn't tempted fate. "You all right?" I ask Harper.

She straightens. "Yeah, I'm fine. Let's get going. We've got to find water while there's still daylight."

Sofia's looking at Harper's hand with a fixed stare. "What's that on your palm?" she asks.

The mold has left an orange goo on her skin. Harper swipes at it, growing frantic when the goo leaves angry-looking hives. "Damn it," she swears, her face grimacing in pain. In about five minutes, she can't move her arm. Her skin turns blue with alarming speed.

Sofia swears in Spanish and roots through her bag. "Epinephrine," she mutters. "I know I have some in here."

Harper drops to the ground, gasping for breath. "We need to put something under her," I order Ryanna. "Don't let the grass touch her bare skin. We don't know if it is toxic." Shit. *Shit.* Even if Sofia can stop the allergic reaction, Harper's not going to be in any shape to walk. We're three hours away from the ship. I don't know what to do.

Sofia breaks the seal and stabs the needle in Harper's thigh. I make a split-second decision. "I'm going to run ahead and look for water. Sofia, Ryanna, the two of you need to get Harper back to the ship. Put her in stasis. I'll be back as soon as I can."

Ryanna looks up, her black eyes shining with fear. "I can come with you."

"No, Sofia can't manage Harper on her own." I press Beirax's weapon into her hand. "I'll be fine."

Hopefully.

I continue for another hour, my heart pounding in my chest. The heat is sweltering, but I'm still grateful for the long sleeved space suit. After what happened to Harper, I can't risk brushing my bare skin against the vegetation.

My head aches and my throat is parched. I'm sorely tempted to reach for the berries that hang from the yellow-leaved bushes, but I know how foolish that urge is.

I walk along, one foot in front of another, moving on autopilot. The mountain still looms in front of me, and it doesn't appear any closer than it did four hours ago.

God, it's hot as hell here. My suit is soaked with sweat, and my hair is a frizzy mess.

Good one, Vi. You're on an alien prison planet without food, water, or shelter, and you're thinking about the state of your hair. Like it will matter if an alien appears to eat you. You're not going to charm him with your good looks today.

As I trudge past more trees with orange mold, I start composing my online dating profile. *I like pina coladas and long trips through space. Oh, and as a scientist, I'm extremely interested in alien anatomy.* Wink, wink, nod, nod.

A giggle cuts the humid air. I slap a hand over my mouth when I realize it came from me.

Great. Now you're losing your mind.

I hear a noise—a soft buzzing sound—and pivot on my heels. A creature flies at me, and I scream in fright. It looks like an insect—some kind of red and yellow housefly—except it's as big as a German Shepherd. Four antennas poke out from the top of its head, each ending in a ball that looks oddly like a strawberry.

"Shoo." I wave my arms at it, trying to scare it away. All animals are scared of loud noises and sudden movement, right? I scream again, wishing I hadn't given Ryanna Beirax's weapon.

The dog-insect chirps at me, then it veers off to my right and plunges into the jungle. I'm about to continue on my way when I hear something miraculous.

The sound of running water.

"Good dog, Lassie." Crashing through the brush, I follow the dog insect's trail, and twenty minutes later, I stand at the edge of an immensely wide purple-tinged river. Lassie's twenty feet away, all four strawberry antennas immersed in the water as she drinks.

For all of three seconds, I hesitate, wondering if the water's safe, and then I fling caution to the wind. If I can't quench my thirst, my odds of survival are zero. I have no choice.

I cup some water in my hands and tip it down my throat. It's cool and clear and ever-so-slightly sweet, and I don't think I've ever tasted anything so delicious in my life. I dip my hands into the river again, eager for more.

I'm so busy drinking that I don't notice the three animals until they're almost on me. They look like wild jackals, with golden and black striped fur, but they're the size of ponies, and their mouths are filled with sharp, jagged teeth.

As I back up, they stand on their hind legs and hoot in unison. Their front claws extend, and they close in on me. I'm hemmed in between the lake and the predators. There's nowhere to go. Nowhere to escape.

I'm going to die on the prison planet.

4

NYX

As soon as we hear the hoots of the Dwals, we begin to run. Of all the creatures we've encountered in this world, the Dwals are the most dangerous. They're smart, vicious hunters. They hoot when they've found prey, and they will attack any moment now.

As I run, I think about Arax's words yesterday. I shouldn't have asked him about the Draekon mutation. The subject has to be a painful one for my friend. Once the Firstborn of Zoraht, he was in line to rule the Zorahn Empire, until the mutant gene was discovered in his body.

A thief on the streets of Vissa does not have much use for the Highborn of Zoraht, but Arax has earned my respect.

As much as I scoff at the notion that the Highborn are meant to rule, Arax is a born leader. It was Arax who kept us motivated in the initial months of despair. Arax who led search parties for food, for water, for any signs of habitation. It was Arax who made us cut down the *kunnr* trees to create a compound wall, Arax who planned the annual migration to the high cliffs during the rainy season. Now, it's Arax who runs to the object that crashed from the sky, hope powering his muscles.

Do I dare hope as well? If it is a spaceship that has crashed on the prison planet, perhaps it can be fixed. Perhaps we can finally escape from this long, lonely exile. I dream about civilization every night, of sinking into the softness of a woman's embrace, smelling the perfume of her flesh, feeling her body tighten against mine as we move in an age-old dance.

We can't return to Zoraht; I'm not a fool. Fear of the Draekon mutation runs too deep for us ever to be able to step foot on my homeworld. But there are other planets outside the control of the High Emperor, worlds in which we could live in the shadows, finding work as mercenary warriors.

Then I calculate the odds of the spaceship surviving the landing, and hope fades.

This part of the prison planet is not unfamiliar to me. While we typically hunt to the east of the Na'Lung cliffs, we've ventured west of the peaks before. The medicinal herbs that Vulrux needs for his potions can only be found in the dense jungle that packs the lowlands in this part of the world, and I've journeyed through the thick vegetation at least a dozen times.

"The Dwals attack on the banks of the river," Arax says, as familiar with the terrain as I am.

We're nearing the water now. I reach for my twin knives, carved painstakingly from the thighbone of a Gawi. At my side, Arax does the same with grim determination. The Dwals are formidable predators, and this will be a harshly-fought battle.

We round a corner, and I see the creature that the Dwals

have surrounded. It is small with dark hair. Its face is strangely unmarked, but its body is curved and lush.

It looks like a woman.

But it cannot be. That's not possible. What on Vissa is a woman doing on the prison planet? The Draekon mutation has never been found in a female. Only men are susceptible.

My thoughts fragmented and confused, I drop to a knee and throw the knife in my right hand. It flies straight and true and lands with unerring accuracy into the chest of the *dwal* closest to the woman. Arax's weapon follows a heartbeat later, piercing it between the eyes. The creature howls in pain and falls to the ground.

The woman looks up for the first time, and her eyes fall on us.

When her gaze locks with mine, there's an instant of quiet. The air grows heavier. The world comes to a standstill, and a voice inside my soul hums in satisfaction. *Her,* it seems to say. *Our mate.*

I barely have time to absorb that shock when an excruciating pain fills my body. Heat ripples down my back. I cry out as my skin rips open. My muscles lock, and I fall to my hands and knees.

Besides me, Arax does the same, his face contorting in agony.

My nails lengthen into claws. My skin changes, stretches, becomes hard and unyielding, a cross between scales and leather. I bellow, and the sound comes as a raw blast, my face twisting, jaw reshaping.

I rear up, and something slices open my back. Writhing in pain, I turn my head on a too-long neck to see spiky vertebrae form on my spine and wings erupt from my lower back. And I have a tail, long and leathery, with a barb at the end. It lashes to and fro.

The cloud of agony clears. The air around me is crisp and chill, but my body burns. I tower over the river, my head at the level of the tallest tree. The water at my feet reflects a huge, scaly body, long neck, and wedge-shaped head with ridges along the forehead.

I am no longer a man. Long ago, one of my father's friends stole an ancient tapestry, and woven into it was an image of a creature, large and dangerous. I see that image now, reflected in the pool in front of me.

I've become a monster.

Yesssss. The creature inside me hisses. *We are free.*

The two remaining Dwals are frozen at the sight of the transformation, but when I rise on four feet, they are spurred to attack. They take a threatening step toward me, their claws fully extended, their jaws open in a snarl, hooting softly to each other.

At my side, a crimson dragon rears on its hind legs. *Arax.*

I blink. Golden threads seem to run between my body and his, and link us to a third. The fragile woman standing ankle deep in the river. *Our mate,* that voice in my soul repeats.

My wings unfurl from my back. A roar builds in my chest. Rivers of rage run through my blood. The beast in me acts on instinct. The Dwals dare attack our mate? I will destroy them.

Almost as one, Arax and I open our mouths and exhale, and we breathe a pure golden fire that burns the attacking Dwals to a crisp.

Our mate's wild gaze darts from us to the charred, blackened remains of the predators that attacked her. Then, she slowly crumples into a dead faint.

The instant she loses consciousness, the thread connecting the three of us seems to snap. A moment of blackness, and I am lying stunned on the ground. When I rise to my feet, I am, once again, a man.

The woman's legs are turning purple, the stain of the *kilpei* poison spreading over her skin.

Blast. This is bad. The *kilpei* can sometimes cause comas. She might even die.

Our mate, the beast inside me insists. *Keep her safe.*

The grass rustles around us. More Dwals, in all likelihood. We need to get out of here.

I sling the woman over my shoulder, and I begin to run for the safety of the caves at the base of the Na'Lung cliffs.

5

VIOLA

With a sigh of relief, I realize I must be dreaming.

My skin feels prickly, my body is feverish, and my throat hurts. My stomach aches with hunger, and I can't remember when I last ate. *On Earth,* a voice in my head says helpfully. *Five days ago.*

That thought should worry me, but since I'm clearly in the middle of a dream, I keep my eyes closed and allow the images to flicker through my head.

I'm surrounded by three massive wild animals with large fangs and vicious-looking claws. They advance on me. I'm trapped between the river and the predators, with nowhere to run. I step back until water swirls around my ankles, but something pricks my skin, and I stop, not daring to wade into the river further and risk getting bitten again.

Two men run toward me at full speed, holding wickedly curved knives with serrated blades in their hands. In unison, they throw them. The weapons slice into the creature closest to me, and it crumples to the ground, dead.

When I see them, wild exultation fills my head. My

heart hammers in my chest, and I can't tear my eyes away from my rescuers.

Both men are seven feet tall. They wear crimson loincloths and nothing else. Their forearms are covered with black tattoos. One has shoulder-length hair, and the other's is shorter and chestnut brown. Their bodies are chiseled muscled perfection. Their chests are streaked with swirled indigo markings, and their nipples are pierced with red barbells.

My insides clench, hard. The pounding in my head increases, and it's getting difficult to breathe.

Focus, Vi.

Other than their height and coloring, they look human. A little Conan-the-Barbarian in their fashion sense, but if they're friendly, I can deal with all the hard, rippling muscles on display.

Oh yeah.

I wasted so much time staring at the Prison Planet hotties, I forgot about the fact that three tiger-like things were about to attack. The two remaining predators move closer to me, swiping their claws in my direction.

Then something surreal happens. The men fall to their knees, and they *change.* As I watch, their bodies morph and distort. Their loincloths rip, exposing their large veiny cocks, bronze in color, each thicker than my wrist and more than ten inches long.

I'm so fascinated by their umm, equipment, that I almost miss the main event. The two men in front of me are transforming into dragons. Yup. The mythical creatures that aren't supposed to exist. Claws, scales, fangs, tails, and huge, leathery wings. When the tiger-dog-animals snarl, the dragons rise, their long scaly necks adding several feet to their already towering height.

Even as beasts, I can see the rage in their eyes. Fear grips my heart as they swing their giant heads toward me, and open their jaws. A sheet of flame erupts from them, burning the creatures on either side of me to nothingness.

I can still feel the heat from the fire on my skin.

If it's a dream, should you be able to feel? The voice inside me asks pointedly.

Of course it's a dream, I reply. *Men cannot turn into dragons. That's impossible.*

Blackness descends.

A heartbeat later, I'm being carried through the jungle, thrown over the broad shoulder of one of the men like a sack of potatoes. He's running, and each time his feet hit the ground, a shock goes through my head. *This isn't a very good part of the dream.* It feels like someone's sticking a hot poker in my eye. *Maybe I should wake up.*

But it's not just my head that hurts. My right ankle feels like it's on fire, and it seems easier to sleep. I close my eyes and allow myself to drift off.

When awareness returns, I'm lying on the ground, naked. My skin burns and throbs. My mind feels foggy, and every time I draw breath, pain fills my lungs.

The dark-haired alien is leaning toward me, his lips inches from mine. I want to reach for him, *for both of them.* There's a throbbing in my sex, a wanton, insistent heat that begs for their touch. The layers of civilization have been stripped away, and what's left is raw, primitive lust.

Dream Viola is a lot more brazen than the real Viola.

"She's reacting badly to the kilpei."

Translating Old-Zor to English, my earpiece pipes up. *Inaccuracies may occur.*

It's weird that the translator is working in my dream.

My brain feels like it's submerged in a tub of molasses. "Who are you?" I croak out.

They ignore my words and bend over me, worry etched in their faces. "We've got to soothe the rash, Arax," the dark-haired one says.

The man with the shoulder-length hair is Arax then. That's a nice name. "Hello," I say again. "I'm right here. My name is Viola Lewis. It's nice to meet you, I think. Unless you're going to burn me with that crazy dragon fire shit."

You're babbling, Vi, a small, coherent part of my mind says. *There's a toxin in your blood. Something on this planet attacked you. Just like Harper. You're going into a coma.*

Arax gazes long and deep into my eyes, and my heartbeat speeds up. His eyes are sea-blue in color, and a woman could drown in their depths. "It's spreading fast," he says. "We need to suck the kilpei out."

Wait, what?

Getting on their knees, they pick up an ankle each. Their lips lock onto my burning flesh and suck hard. My skin tingles at their touch, and a welcoming coolness spreads through me.

Yeah. I'm definitely dreaming, and while I've had some strange dreams before, this one takes the cake. It's been a while since I've been with a man, and my subconscious must be telling me to get some nookie, because why else would I imagine two aliens licking every inch of my body?

Whatever you do, Vi, don't wake up.

Their tongues caress a path up my body. My legs quiver, but they ignore the target between my thighs and continue up my bare hips, mouths sealed on my flesh, following the purple rash up my torso.

My hands fall to caress their heads. One of the men, the dark-haired one whose name I don't know, looks at me intently, his eyes blazing with desire. The heat in his gaze makes me gasp, and I let my hands fall away. I'm going to die. If not from the strange discoloration on my skin, then from explosive lust.

The men's mouths move to my breasts, and they suck on my nipples. I stifle a moan and writhe on the floor. *Maybe it's not polite for me to orgasm while they're saving my life?* They nibble kisses down every inch of my body, and everywhere their mouths land, my skin loses its fevered, prickly feeling.

"It's working." Arax's voice fills with relief. "The kilpei is receding."

The dark-haired man's mouth meets mine in a soft kiss. The burning prickliness is replaced by a different kind of heat, one that makes my core ache with need. I squirm and part my legs, wordlessly begging for more.

Both men inhale sharply, and the dark-haired man pulls away. "The kilpei poison has made you weak," he says gently. "Rest now, *aida*."

The others, I think with a stab. Harper, Ryanna, and Sofia, left to fend for themselves in this dangerous place. Olivia, May, and the other women in stasis. Beirax and Raiht'vi. I should get back to the ship.

Something else nudges at my consciousness. Something important. *Something I'm forgetting...*

But the blanket of sleep presses down on me, firm and insistent, and I can't rouse myself out of my half-slumber. *It's okay, Vi,* I think sleepily, as tendrils of darkness coil over me. *There's nothing to worry about. It's just a dream.*

6

ARAX

The stories were true after all.

"Tell me again," Nyx says, once the woman is asleep, his voice vibrating with anger, "what you know about the Draekon mutation."

There are only three people that have unfettered access to the ThoughtVaults of Zoraht, where the true story of the Draekons is written down. The High Emperor himself, the Firstborn, and the head of the Council of Scientists.

Nyx had no warning.

I lean back against the wall of the cave, my legs stretched in front of me. As Firstborn on Zoraht, I've been trained to keep secrets, but after sixty years in exile, it's finally time to let some of them go. "Twelve hundred years ago," I begin, "the scientists created the Draekons, a race of invincible warriors with the ability to shift into dragons."

"Like we just did."

I nod. "The scientists intended for the Draekons to be sterile."

Nyx surveys me with his dark eyes. "The beast inside

me," he says, "insists that this woman is my mate. Our mate."

Not just the beast inside Nyx. The beast inside me rages at me, demanding that I claim the woman. *She is ours,* it says. *We must take her. We must complete the bond.*

"Something went wrong," I reply. "The gene mutated. Each mutation gave the Draekon race more power, and finally the ability to mate. But," I swallow before I explain this next part, "for some reason—maybe because compatible females were few and far between—instead of a pair bond, Draekons form a triad."

"A triad?" Nyx raises a brow.

"Two Draekons mate one woman."

Nyx is silent for a very long time, examining his fingernails as if remembering them turning into claws. I resist the urge to do the same. Wonder still courses through me over the way our bodies morphed into such powerful creatures.

My skin tingles pleasantly when I look at the soft woman beside us. I rise and turn away, and it grows stronger, almost painful.

So the legends are true. The Draekons are tainted with darkness.

My mouth goes dry with fear. "My dragon," I say, through stiff lips, placing a hand on my chest where the buzzing is the worst. "It wants to mate."

Nyx's brow creases. He looks from me to the woman, and rises as well, his hand over his chest. "I feel it, too." His expression changes from wonder to horror. "This is why they sent us away," he says quietly. "Are we animals, Arax? Do we fall on the woman and rut her, the way the beast inside me demands I do?"

I clench my hands into fists, willing the tingling to dissipate. When it does not, I center my mind as I was taught, and relief pours through me as the desperate need ebbs. The buzzing desire is there, but it is in the background, an annoying insect.

I want to pick our mate up, hold her and cradle her against my body, but I force back that need. The man in me will not take what is not freely offered, even though the dragon inside me yearns for the bonding to be complete. I will not force our mate.

"No." I'm feeling the same storm of emotions that Nyx is. Even though we've been on this planet for sixty seasons, even though we've been forced to live in exile without the comfort of a woman's touch, I'm not ready to surrender to the wild animal that prowls inside me. "I will not do that. Not while the man in me still has control."

The ThoughtVaults speak of a Draekon rebellion and its swift, brutal suppression. When the Zorahn realized that their creations could turn against them, Kannix, High Emperor of Zoraht, ordered the scientists to create a disease that would eradicate the Draekons. *And it was done.*

An entire generation of Draekon warriors died, as did their offspring.

The Draekons were exterminated because they lost control. I cannot allow my resolve to weaken. Then Nyx asks the most important question, the one I haven't yet answered.

"How do you transform into the beast?" He asks pensively. "Is it in the presence of imminent danger?"

Nyx isn't going to like my answer.

"No." I take a deep breath and recite the relevant passage from the ThoughtVaults. "An unmated Draekon shifts into the beast for the first time when he recognizes his mate. After that first shift, the Draekon is trapped and cannot shift until the bonding is complete."

I lift my head up and meet his gaze squarely. "The creature inside wants to be free, Nyx. It rages at us to mate now, and the pressure's only going to get worse as time goes on."

"You're telling me," he says slowly, putting the pieces of the puzzle together, "that sooner or later, the dragon will take over."

I nod heavily. "Sooner or later," I say, "we're going to have to mate with her. There is no choice."

7

VIOLA

I'm not dreaming.

The two alien men who turned into dragons are sitting at the mouth of the cave, talking quietly. When I hear their words, I freeze.

Sooner or later, we're going to have to mate with her. There is no choice.

That's when a bunch of realizations crash into me, things I should have figured out earlier, but didn't, thanks to the *kilpei*.

These two men are Draekons. The fearsome beasts that Raiht'vi warned us about. What did she say, back on the ship? *The Draekons are dangerous. Not to be trusted.*

Next realization? They're talking about me. They mean to mate with me. The two of them. And I won't have any choice in the matter because if I fight back, they'll probably turn into dragons and burn me to a crisp.

It wasn't until I was an adult that I realized that the wolf in Little Red Riding Hood was an allegory. It wasn't a real wolf that Red needed to be afraid of. No, the danger came from strange men who would take her against her will. *Is this what Raiht'vi was warning me about?*

I thought crash-landing on a jungle planet was bad. Turns out I jumped from the frying pan into the fire.

Think, Vi, think. What are you going to do?

There's a moment of silence, and one of them turns his head toward me. I hold my breath and wonder if they'll figure out I'm awake, but I get lucky because they continue their conversation. "The object we saw must have been a ship," Arax says. "How else could she have got here?"

"It's the only explanation that makes sense," the other alien agrees. "It must be within a day's walk of here. Tomorrow morning, I'll go looking for it."

"I'm not sure if that's a good idea, Nyx," Arax says. "Uzzan is shrouded tonight. The rainy season is almost on us. We need to hunt before the lowlands flood."

The rainy season is approaching, and the lowlands will flood.

That's not good.

As best as I can tell, our ship is smack dab in the middle of the lowlands. Visions of rain pouring through the ship run through my mind. The water level rising, seeping into the stasis pods, drowning the others in their sleep... *Stop that, Vi,* I tell myself sternly. *There's no point imagining the worst case scenario.*

But is that truly the worst-case scenario? These two alien dragon-men intend to mate with me. What happens when they find out there are eight other women on board the *Fehrat 1*?

Nothing good, I'm prepared to bet.

Here's what you need to do, Vi. Distract them from searching for the ship. Don't tell them about the other women, and at the first chance you get, escape back to the safety of *Fehrat 1*, and hope like hell that the High Emperor of Zoraht has sent a rescue party.

It's not much of a plan, but it's all I've got.

IT IS dark when I wake again. The temperature has cooled with the setting of the sun, and it is no longer stifling hot. I'm still naked. Instinctively, I grope for my top, but it's nowhere in reach.

I drag myself to a sitting position. I'm as weak as a kitten. My head throbs, and my body feels like it's been hit with a battering ram. And despite my aches and pains, my nipples are hard, and my insides are slippery. What the heck is wrong with me? I must have hit my head when we crashed, because there's no other explanation for this level of stupidity.

My movements have roused the two alien men. The dark-haired man, Nyx, is at my side in a second. "Drink, *aida*," he says, holding a curved leather sac to my lips. Maybe I'm trying to keep myself from panicking, but in the dim light of the twin moons, I imagine that his eyes are kind.

My throat is parched, and I don't bother asking if it's safe. Right now, being poisoned is the least of my worries, so I drink deeply from the vessel.

Arax watches me, his face wary. "Who are you?" he asks me as soon as I put down the water sac. "Where are you from?"

I should answer, I know, but I can't stop thinking about their cocks. Earlier, right before they'd transformed into dragons, they'd been erect and extremely impressive. Nyx isn't hard now, but the bulge underneath his loincloth still makes me swallow a gulp.

You're a fool, Vi. A horny, can't-stop-staring-at-alien-junk fool.

Nyx notices my gaze, and his lips curve into a cocky smile. The expression is very human and pretty damn irresistible. "You want to feel me between your legs, *aida*?" he asks. "The beast inside me hungers for you. It snarls, and it howls at me, demanding that Arax and I take you, bond with you and fulfill our destiny." His eyes rake over my naked body. "Ask me to sink into you and I will," he says huskily. "All you have to do is ask."

Whoa there, buddy. Buy me dinner first.

Then again, who am I kidding? My body throbs under Nyx's gaze. My nipples harden, and my pussy grows heavy, and I want to part my legs and feel his hard length thrust into my body. I might not understand the intensity of my need, but I can't deny it.

Unlike Nyx, Arax's expression stays stern. "Answer me," he demands, his voice cold. "What do you want with us?"

His tone shocks the lust out of me. I scramble to my feet, my fingers searching in the darkness for my space suit. "I don't want anything from you."

To my horror, I feel my eyes fill with tears. I'm on an alien planet. So far, I've been snarled at by three terrifying beasts, watched the two aliens in front of me transform into dragons, and nearly died when something bit me in the water. My belly rumbles with hunger. My skin feels fragile and paper-thin. My head still throbs in pain. I'm panicking at the idea that these dragons are going to mate with me, and I'm terrified that I'm never going to see Earth again.

Then there's Harper, Sofia, and Ryanna. The possibility of the three women running into the wild jackal-horse things that almost killed me sends shivers of horror through my body. For my own sanity, I have to assume they made it back to the safety of the ship. "I just want to go home," I say with a sniff, wiping the tears away with the back of my hand. "That's all."

Of course, they don't understand a word I say.

Though their faces soften with sympathy at the sight of my tears, their expressions are confused. "What did she say?" Nyx asks Arax. "Can you understand her?"

I want to smack myself on the head. I have a translator in my ear, but of course, these aliens do not. I'm about to scream in frustration when I remember that I raided the Zorahn ship before we left. Didn't I take a couple of translators? Pulling my pants over my legs, I stick my hands in my pockets, and to my utter relief, my fingers close over the three earpieces. "Oh thank heavens," I whisper, holding them out to the aliens.

They take them from me with narrowed eyes. Exchanging glances with each other, they stick the translators in their ears. If the electric shock bothers them, they show no sign of it.

I shove my hands back in my pockets and cross my fingers. "Can you understand me now?"

8

NYX

Our mate has a Zorahn translator. Less than a knur ago, I thought Arax was being too suspicious. Now, I'm not so sure. Could this lovely, frail female be a spy for the Zorahn authorities?

Even if she is, that's no excuse for snapping at her. The creature inside me rages at Arax. *She is our mate,* it fumes. *We should cherish her, not growl at her.*

For once, I'm in full agreement with it. "Yes," I reply, taking care to keep my voice gentle. "We understand you."

She exhales in relief. "Thank heavens," she murmurs, her voice sweet and low.

Heaven is similar in concept to Caeron, the translator informs me. *The people of Earth believe in two separate Caerons. One for the good, one for the bad.*

It's a strange belief. What's more important is that she's from somewhere called Earth, and I've never heard of it. They make you learn the names of the discovered worlds in Primary. I've memorized the list; this planet that our mate speaks of is not on it.

"My name is Viola Lewis," she continues, her mouth stretching into a tentative smile. "Hi."

That smile gives me hope. She's not backed up against the walls of the cave. She's not screaming with fear. She doesn't look terrified.

Out of the corner of my eye, I see Arax open his mouth, his expression troubled. The Firstborn thinks that this alien woman is a threat to our existence, and his first instinct is always to protect. Whatever his beast desires, Arax will never ignore his duty.

I'm not Highborn. The scientists exiled us to an uninhabited planet and left us to die. For sixty seasons, we haven't seen a woman. I don't care how much of a threat she is.

We have found our mate.

For the first time in a very long time, I feel alive. I am complete.

Before he can continue his line of questioning about the circumstances that lead Viola Lewis to the prison planet, I jump in, giving Arax a quelling glance. *The interrogation can wait.* "Viola Lewis," I say out loud, trying the strange words on my tongue. I remember how frightening this world was when we first got here, and there were fourteen of us. Viola Lewis was alone when we found her, with no weapon to defend herself. It's a miracle that she's not huddled in a corner, gibbering with terror. "I am Nyx, and this is Arax."

"Nyx," she repeats. "Arax. Thank you for rescuing me from the scary dog-jackal things."

"Dwals." I smile at her. "They lurk near the water, looking for easy prey."

She shudders. "They almost found it," she says. "If you two hadn't shown up, I'd have been Dwals lunch."

"Lunch?" I snort in amusement. "You're too little for that, Viola Lewis. You would have been a tasty snack."

Her skin turns pink. "Then you licked me," she says. Another shiver runs through her, but this time, her eyes rake over our bodies, and her scent is one of arousal, not fear.

Arax's lips curl into a smile. "You were stung by a *kilpei* plant," he explains. "We had to soothe the rash that was spreading over your skin."

"By licking me?"

Arax's eyes twinkle. "You appeared to enjoy it."

She flushes again. "And of course, there's the elephant in the room. You're dragons."

"We are Draekon," Arax corrects her. "Twelve hundred years ago, Zorahn scientists created a warrior race with the ability to morph from man to dragon. They were meant to be the perfect soldier-slaves, but eventually, the scientists lost control. The Draekons rampaged." He stares into the distance. "In the homeworld, every male is tested yearly. If we are found with the mutation, we are exiled."

Arax's frankness surprises me. For sixty seasons, the Firstborn kept the knowledge he'd learned in the Thought-Vaults secret from us, but he does not hesitate to share information with Viola Lewis.

The beast inside me purrs approvingly. *We have no secrets from our mate.*

Viola Lewis leans forward, her face glowing in Uzzan's faint light. "That's why you were exiled?" she asks, sounding shocked. She chews at her lower lip, looking like she's waging a battle with herself. "You asked me what I'm doing here. I'm from a planet called Earth. Six months ago, space-ships landed from the sky."

"Zorahn spaceships?"

She nods. Before she can continue her story, her stomach rumbles with hunger. Remorse fills me, and I curse myself for being a thoughtless fool. I open my pack and pull some *kunnr* fruit out. I slice it for her with my throwing knife. "Eat, *aida*."

"Can I? Will I react to it?"

It's a new sensation, having a second set of instincts inside me. Somehow I know the fruit will not hurt our mate. "I do not sense danger."

"All right," she says with a shrug. "I have to eat some-time. If it causes a reaction, I guess you can perform mouth-to-mouth." She mutters the last few words, and I do not know what they mean, but the flush on her cheeks is unmistakable.

Ask us, aida. All you have to do is ask for what you want.

She reaches for my offering and takes an experimental nibble. "Tastes like... *vanilla pudding*," she says, her face surprised. I don't know what *vanilla pudding* is, but she seems to like the fruit, so I cut her another piece, and she eats quickly, licking her fingers to catch all the juice. My cock throbs, aching for her. *Take her,* the beast rumbles in my chest, insistent, demanding. *She is ours.*

"Where did I leave off?" she asks. "Until the Zorahn appeared, we thought we were alone in the universe."

Alone? The galaxy teems with life. Earth must be a very isolated planet.

"The Zorahn cured us of disease," she continues, her tone is tinged with a sadness that I don't understand. "They asked us for help in return. A sickness was spreading across Zoraht, and the scientists didn't know how to cure it. They wanted volunteers to travel to Zoraht and participate in a medical study of some kind." Her lips twist in a wry smile. "So I did."

I offer her another piece of *kunnr*, and she takes it from me with a murmur of thanks.

I frown. "You left your planet alone to travel to a strange world? What of your clansmen?"

Arax lights a fire in the middle of the cave as he listens to her story, and he cooks a piece of salted *hulundi* over the flames. The large fish is plentiful in the waters on this planet, and it makes for tasty eating. It was one of the first foods we discovered when we were first exiled.

"I don't have any." She sounds forlorn, and I want to take her into my arms and soothe away her pain. *We are her mates. She will never be alone again.* "It was only for six months, and the Zorahn swore we would be safe. High Emperor Lenox guaranteed it."

Arax's expression turns grim. If Lenox is High Emperor, it means that Arax's father, the High Emperor Dravex, is dead. "I'm sorry," I say quietly to my friend.

"It was expected," he replies flatly.

It sounds like Arax doesn't care about the death of his father, but I know better. The Firstborn is hurting inside, but he is Highborn, and he will not let his grief show.

He focuses his attention on the fire. When the fish is ready, he turns to our mate and hands her a piece of the *hulundi*, his gaze softening when he looks at her. "It's safe to eat," he assures her.

"I'll take your word for it." She nibbles questioningly, pleasure filling her face as she tastes the fish.

"How many Earth women did the scientists recruit? How many were on board the ship?" he asks.

Her body stiffens almost imperceptibly. "There were ten of us, and three Zorahn," she says. "I'm the only survivor."

I watch her. The tension in her body, the slight shift of her eyes, the tightness of her voice... My senses tingle.

I'm the son of a thief. I can tell when someone isn't being truthful.

For some reason of her own, Viola Lewis is lying to us.

The answers will lie in the wreckage of the ship. When the sun rises in the morning, I intend on finding the truth.

9

VIOLA

On the one hand, Arax and Nyx have both been nice to me. They saved me from the Dwals. They fed me. Despite the whole *'we're going to have to mate with her; there is no choice'* bit, they haven't jumped me.

On the other hand, Raiht'vi's warnings echo in my mind. She'd been terrified by the Draekons. So had Mannix. If the massive, hulking Zorahn are freaking out, shouldn't I be doing the same thing?

I don't know who to trust. I don't know what to do. It would be a lot easier to think if I wasn't so distracted by the incredibly hot alien men.

For the last five years, my father's illness was my only priority. Getting him to the hospital, taking care of him during chemotherapy, watching as the cancerous cells took over his body until he wasted away and died... Dating took a back seat.

Men have been absent from my life for a very long time.

All that pent-up celibacy is overflowing now. A voice in the back of my head tells me I'm being foolish, but for some reason, I can't bring myself to care. I ache for the aliens in front of me. My sex throbs for them. I want to reach out and touch their hard, bronzed cocks, and I want to spread my legs and let them take me. Both of them.

Earth to Viola. You're stranded on an alien planet. Can you maybe drag your mind out of the gutter long enough to try and make some kind of plan?

"They're all dead?" Arax asks me, his voice layered with skepticism. "Everyone on the ship except you, and you're unscathed?"

I have a split-second to react. A split-second to make a choice. *Trust Raiht'vi or trust the Draekons?*

My instincts tell me I have nothing to fear from Arax and Nyx. But I'm not sure it matters. My instincts have been wrong before. When my dad was first diagnosed with cancer, I was convinced he'd beat it.

He's dead now. So much for womanly intuition.

We're on an alien planet. Bright orange fungi—fluffy and harmless looking—can kill me. I'm horny for no apparent reason. In such a strange and hostile environment, I'm not sure I can trust myself.

Raiht'vi was badly wounded in the crash. She's possibly dying. There's no reason for her to mislead us.

Arax is staring at me, waiting for me to answer. I take a deep breath and double-down on the lies. "Yes, they're all dead." I think of poor Janet, and I don't have to fake the tears that gather in my eyes. I blink them away. *Now's not the time to melt down, Vi. Hold it together.*

Sensing my distress, Arax gathers me into his arms. His face softens. "You're safe now," he murmurs. "Nothing will hurt you. I give you my word, Viola Lewis."

I lean against his broad chest. Is it wrong to enjoy being held so much? In Arax's arms, I feel soothed. This is the first time I've felt truly secure on this alien planet.

Scratch that. This is the first time I feel safe since my dad got ill.

You're not being wise, Vi.

"You said there were three Zorahn," Nyx probes. "They're dead too?"

I nod again, unable to meet the dark-haired alien's eyes. He doesn't look convinced. Shit. Should I come clean?

Before I can think through my best course of action, Nyx speaks again. "In the morning," he says, surveying me thoughtfully, "I'm going to look for the wreckage of the spaceship. If nothing else, the metal will be useful for weapons."

Crap on a cracker. The instant they find the spaceship, my lies will be exposed.

Raiht'vi's warning rings in my ears. *The Draekons are dangerous.*

I need a distraction. Something to get their minds off the mysterious circumstances of my arrival on this planet.

Something big.

And I have only one tool at my disposal. Sex.

They want to mate with me.

Truth be told, the desire isn't one-sided. Lust burns in my blood. It's been an insistent undertone from the first moment I saw them. I can't help wondering what it would feel like to be with them. Their cocks are massive. One of them is too large for me. Two of them?

Color me intrigued. And seriously turned on.

Before my courage abandons me, I inch even closer to Arax. My skin prickles in arousal, and my body heats. I run my thumb over his pierced nipple, and he inhales sharply. I lift my face up to him and wrap my arm around his neck. "Kiss me again," I breathe. "Both of you."

Then I place my lips over his.

I'm in control for a moment, coaxing his mouth open with an encouraging murmur.

He tastes delicious, smoke and heat. I start to ponder the carcinogenic effects of dragon fire, and then I have no time to laugh or ponder, because Arax seizes me, one large hand coming to grip my neck and hold me still.

He plunders my mouth, pulling moans from deep within my chest. His other hand brushes the line of my jaw, his touch tender. Meanwhile, his tongue explores me, alternating hard, dueling thrusts with coaxing caresses, making me wonder if this is the sort of lover he will be—perfect, powerful, and brutal. I clutch him tighter, wishing I could pull my body into his. He tugs my hair gently, breaking our mouths apart for a moment.

"*Aida*," he whispers, his eyes hazy with desire, and I am lost.

My body is already trembling on the edge of orgasm. Another word, another touch and I'll spill over the edge.

Whoa. He almost made the earth move for me with one kiss.

Strong arms wrap around me from behind—Nyx making his move. Where Arax is possessive, Nyx's approach is more subtle. He places little kisses up my spine and sensitive neck and coaxes me back toward him, so I rest on his lap with Arax in front of me.

Seated firmly on Nyx's throbbing cock, I get a front row seat to Arax's strip show. He rips off his loincloth, exposing all of him—and there is a lot of him to take in. I thought his cock was big before, but it's grown even bigger now, long, bronze and lickable.

My pussy throbs in anticipation. My nipples bead as he takes hold of his, er, *foot long*, and slides his hand down to collect the thick moisture beading at the tip. He spreads the liquid over himself until he's fully hard and shiny, all the while never taking his eyes off me.

My arousal, already in the red zone, shoots up a thousand percent.

But I'm not going to lie. As turned on as I am, I don't see how his cock is going to fit in me. It's just too damn big.

Arax tilts his head to the side. "What's the matter?"

"You're huge," I tell him. "This is not going to work."

"You have nothing to fear, Viola Lewis. I assure you, we are compatible. *In every way.*"

"Mmm, talk dirty to me," I murmur. Hey, I joke when I'm nervous. It's what I do.

Nyx huffs a laugh into my hair. "Less talking," he says. "More doing." His fingers quest down my arm to stroke the side of my breast.

I arch my back against him, sighing with pleasure as his fingers brush against my sensitive nipples.

"You like that?" Nyx's voice tickles my ear. His arms cage me, capturing my wrists and pulling my hands away, leaving my breasts exposed to Arax's intent gaze.

"I'm going to touch you, *aida*," Arax says, raw need on his face. Letting go of his cock, he cups my breasts and thumbs the hardened nubs. Bowing his head, he flicks his tongue against my nipples.

The sensation shoots right to my sex. "Oh God, yes. That's it." My body goes taut as a bow. I try to squirm away from Nyx's hold, but the dark-haired alien doesn't budge.

"Should I stop, sweet one?" Arax's eyes go hooded, and I sense the predator lurking inside.

If they stop what they're doing, I will die. I shake my head. "It's just...too much stimulation."

"Too much?" Nyx breathes in my ear. "Or not enough?"

He runs his tongue along the edge of my ear, and I retaliate by grinding my bottom against him. From the pleased purring noise he makes, he enjoys my makeshift lap dance.

Arax's head dips, his hair brushing my collarbone as he nuzzles me. His tongue swipes playful circles around my areolas; torturing and tasting me as he tests my responses. Every so often he pulls away, and Nyx takes over, pinning my arms in such a way that leaves his hands free to pluck my nipples, while Arax studies each of my twitches and moans as if memorizing them.

"She's almost ready to peak," Arax tells Nyx. "I think we should help her, don't you?"

"We should," Nyx agrees, his voice a dark rumble in his chest, sending a shiver of pleasure through me.

I *am* almost ready to peak, as the two hot aliens ravaging my body put it, but before I surrender completely to my orgasm, I need to do a little groping of my own. Common sense has fled the cave. Ever since I saw their cocks for the first time, I've been aching to touch them. "I want to play," I insist, freeing a hand and slipping it underneath me. I find the hard bar of Nyx's cock and squeeze.

He groans in my ear, and his legs tense underneath me. "I don't think so, *aida,*" he says, his voice ragged. "Arax is right. You will peak first."

These aliens are bossy.

I growl in frustration. "It's not fair," I gasp. "Two against one."

"Draekon do not concern themselves with fairness," Arax informs me solemnly, but there's smile lurking on the corner of his lips. "Do not fight your need, sweet one. Let me pleasure you."

Arax grabs my feet. The men move me into position, my head cradled in Nyx's lap, my bottom on Arax's loincloth.

The large Zorahn lies down between my legs, his big hands holding my thighs open.

"I will taste you now, Viola Lewis," he says, his blue eyes dark with heat.

"Whoa, now—" I begin, but Arax seals his mouth over my pussy, and I can't remember words anymore.

Nyx strokes my breasts, crooning softly as Arax goes on the hunt for my orgasm. He's a patient man, kissing my inner thighs until they quiver. He licks a trail to my pussy and pauses to breathe deep. "The smell of you drives me wild," he growls.

"Indeed," Nyx agrees, his voice strained. "I can smell her sweetness from here."

Arax's head dips once again between my legs, exploring every inch of my sex in a way that makes my toes curl. He spends what feels like hours lapping at my lower lips, circling my clitoris, dipping into my folds with his tongue, as if trying to imprint the taste of me into his senses. Every time my body knots up, ready to climax—or 'peak,' as they call it—he backs off, planting soft kisses around my aching sex, and nuzzling my inner thighs.

After a while, I realize he's playing with me.

"Arax," I grunt, tugging his hair. Whatever the Draekons might think, this isn't fair. Nobody should be allowed to torture me with so much pleasure.

He looks up, his eyes dancing with mirth. He's laughing at me, damn it. I jerk my hips in obvious invitation. "Now," I insist.

"Do not try to order a Highborn," Nyx says to me, his tone amused. "It's a waste of time. They always get their own way."

Arax's eyebrows rise. "One could say the same of a thief," he murmurs.

"Mmm," Nyx agrees. "Though we have a more efficient approach than the Highborn."

"What?" Arax's tone is outraged. "Thieves sneak in. We choose a full-on attack."

Seriously? I'm lying on the ground, legs spread open, my body on the verge of a climax, and we're chatting about thieves and attacks? Arax is not the only one who's outraged. "Can you guys stop talking strategy and fuck me?" I demand.

Nyx chuckles. Arax's hot breath gusts across my aching sex and I strain to press my pussy against his mouth, failing as he hovers mere inches away.

"Goddammit!" I curse, and when that has no effect, I change tactics. "Please," I beg, throwing my head back and straining my hips up. "Please fuck me."

Arax's tongue thrusts inside my pussy. "Oh, yes," I scream. Nyx grips my right breast, hard and possessive, and my pleasure spikes. I can't hold back. I climax in a series of gasps, my pussy muscles clenching hard.

Arax doesn't stop. His tongue is relentless, licking my juices, teasing my clitoris. Little mews escape my throat as my body quivers with aftershocks from the best orgasm I've ever had.

"My turn," Nyx says. Before I know it, he and Arax have switched places.

"What?" I can't move; I can barely blink. My body has melted into the floor. I may never move again.

Arax pulls me against his broad chest, tips my head toward him, and kisses me deeply. I can taste myself on his lips. "Nyx wishes to pleasure you," he says. "It wouldn't be fair to deny him your sweetness."

"I thought the Draekon don't believe in the notion of fairness."

They chuckle. Nyx prowls closer, kneeling and parting my legs. His fingertips ghost over my clitoris and my pussy clenches. I ache to be filled by their thick, massive shafts.

"Fuck me," I breathe.

"We intend to," Nyx says, stripping naked with a smile so sexy, it should be illegal on all known planets. His cock is as huge as Arax's, thick and hard, bronzed as if a sculptor wanted to immortalize it forever.

"Stroke me, sweet one."

Gladly. Licking my lips, I close my hand around his erection. His shaft is warm and smooth to touch, and when I pump his length, he throws his head back with a groan of need.

"Viola Lewis." He tugs free and pulls me close, and catches my mouth in a kiss. "Soon you will feel me inside you. Arax and I will claim every inch of your body. But first," he tugs on his cock until golden fluid drips from the tip, and he coats his hand with the thick substance.

I can't take my eyes off him. Watching him pump his shaft is such a turn-on that for a second, my vision turns hazy. "What are you doing?"

"Proving Arax right. Thieves *do* like to sneak in where no one expects it."

He sets a slick finger at my asshole.

Whoa there. I rear up in shock, and this time, Arax restrains me. "You've got to be kidding me," I say, my eyes wide. There's two of them. I should have realized this was going to happen, but until the moment when Nyx's finger circled my tight opening, I hadn't even thought about where two cocks would go.

"I'm not jesting, *aida,*" Nyx says calmly. "We intend to pleasure you in every way possible."

"Oh God," I moan. I should be running away, screaming

at the top of my lungs, but I'm not. Something's wrong with me. I must be really twisted because the idea of Arax and Nyx taking my pussy and ass at the same time doesn't fill me with fear. It fills me with heat. Between Arax's hard arms around me, and Nyx's determined finger fluttering at my back door, my pussy is weeping with need. "I've never done this before."

Fire leaps into Nyx's eyes. "Good," he purrs. "We will be your first." The liquid from his cock—the Zorahn equivalent of precum—is thick and sticky. He uses it as lube, probing my back hole with his finger until my body responds, and I push back against him, wordlessly begging for more.

He finger fucks my bottom, each time pressing deeper, stretching the ring of muscle. At first, I squeeze hard, trying to keep him out, but sensation sweeps over me, and I give in to my desire.

"You're too big," I whimper, hoping I'm wrong. "You'll never fit."

"We will prepare you," Arax soothes me, his hand stroking my nipples. "You never need fear us. We will give you only pleasure."

My muscles relax, and Nyx's finger slides inside. He smiles in satisfaction and teases my clitoris with his tongue. I moan, my whole body clenching as my orgasm burns through my body. Lights flash in the corners of my eyes. I try to speak, but my jaw won't work.

Wait. That's not normal. Something's wrong.

Arax bends over me; concern etched into the corners of his mouth. "Viola Lewis?" His voice comes from far away and swirls away into darkness.

10

ARAX

I n the darkness of night, I rage at myself. The kilpei poison hadn't left our mate's system fully. I should have been making sure she wasn't injured. Instead, I kissed her. Tasted her intoxicating sweetness. Craved her touch.

Though the creature inside me aches for the bonding, I reach a decision. In the morning, I will take Viola Lewis to our dwelling atop the Na'Lung cliffs. My cousin Vulrux is a healer; he will tend to our mate. Her safety is my primary concern. Everything else can wait.

Nyx is asleep, and I'm keeping watch when Viola Lewis stirs again. She sits up, rubbing the sleep out of her eyes, and when she sees that I'm awake, she moves next to me. "I fainted again, didn't I?"

She sounds disgusted with herself. "This bothers you?"

"I'm not used to feeling frail and useless," she replies.

I hand her the water sac so she may quench her thirst. "You shouldn't be so hard on yourself, Viola Lewis," I reply soothingly. "Your body is still recovering from the *kilpei* toxin. You can't help your reactions."

She drinks deeply and sits down at my side. "It's not just that," she mutters. "I wouldn't have been able to defend myself against the Dwals either. If you want to know about the impact of rising planet temperatures on the wheat crop, I'm the woman for you. But ask me to get a drink of water on this world, and I'm useless."

The translator tells me that wheat is an edible grain cultivated on Earth. I wrap my arm around her shoulders, and she rests her head against my chest. "Not everyone is a warrior, *aida*," I reply, trying to think of a way to comfort her.

She sighs. "You probably don't even understand why I'm upset. When something threatens you, you can just turn into a dragon and breathe fire on it. No need to be afraid, right?"

I take a deep breath. "We shifted for the first time when the Dwals attacked you."

"What?" She twists her neck around to gape at me. "How? Why?"

Secrecy is second-nature to the Highborn of Zoraht, but Viola Lewis is my mate. *Tell her the truth,* my beast orders. "Draekons shift for the first time when they see their mate."

Her body goes still. "Oh," she says in a whisper. "But both of you became dragons."

"That's the Draekon way. Two Draekons, one mate."

"That's why, earlier..." Her voice trails away as she understands why Nyx and I wanted to claim her at the same time. "Oh wow." Her skin turns pink. "That's kind of kinky, and kind of hot."

My lips twitch. On the homeworld, anything goes, and it's impossible to shock us. Judging by her embarrassment, the people on Earth must be more sexually repressed than the Zorahn.

But she's not running away. She remains nestled at my

side, and her hand rests lightly on my bare thigh. I don't think she's aware that she's stroking me, but she is, and I have to force myself to breathe evenly.

"That's exciting, isn't it?" she asks, her voice a mere whisper. "Now that you've met me, you can turn into dragons whenever you want."

"Not really." It's not like me to be so open with information. I've been taught from birth that knowledge is power, to be guarded and hoarded. "According to the ThoughtVaults, once we sight our mate, our full powers cannot be unlocked until the bond is complete."

Her hand stops its tentative exploration, and her mouth falls open. "Let me see if I've got this right," she says slowly, pulling away from my hold. "In order to become dragons again, you're going to have to sleep with me."

"Yes. Does that terrify you, Viola Lewis?"

11

VIOLA

Something is wrong with me. *They turn into dragons, Viola,* I scold myself. *You should be freaking out. You should not be thinking about their kisses from earlier, and you most certainly shouldn't be wishing you hadn't fainted.*

My pussy throbs with need. Earlier, when I kissed them, I was attracted to them, but now, the ache in my body intensifies. Every rational bone in my body screams at me to pull away, but I stay exactly where I am, my back pressed against Arax's chest.

I wish Nyx would wake up. I'd like to pick up where we left off. When he fingered my ass, I thought I was going to combust from sheer desire. I'd like to do that again, *and more.* I'd like to be completely filled by the two of them.

This is more than the need to distract them from heading to the ship. This feels far more primal. Raw, need rages in my blood. When Arax says mate, a thrill shoots through me. *Where the heck is this lust coming from?*

I don't know how to answer Arax's question. "I overheard what you said to Nyx," I confess. "You said that sooner or later, you're going to have to mate with me."

His eyebrows rise in a very human way. "I wish you hadn't overheard us," he replies, regret etched in his voice.

"Why?" I challenge him. "Are you afraid I'll run away?"

"Terrified," he replies. His eyes dance with amusement for a brief moment, then his mirth fades. "You can't run from a Draekon, Viola Lewis. Especially not your mates." He places a hand on his chest. "I can sense you here."

I should be much warier. But I've been in a crash. I've almost been eaten by fearsome predators. Tomorrow, I will be sensible. Tonight, my walls are well and truly down.

Earlier today, my plan was to lie to them about the other women, and escape the first chance I got. But the more I think about it, the more I second-guess myself. This planet is scary. Threats are everywhere. Deadly *dwals*, poisonous plants, the crazy orange fungus that got Harper, and the imminent flooding of the lowlands.

Arax and Nyx know how to survive on this planet; I sure as hell don't. *Should I confess that I lied to them? Will they be angry?*

It's too much responsibility. If I make the wrong decision —if I trust them and it turns out to be a mistake—I'm not just putting myself at risk. I'm endangering the others.

I've stayed silent too long. Arax is giving me a questioning look. I trace the outline of a tattoo on his bicep. "Do the markings have significance?" I ask him. "The Zorahn on the ship had them too. Except for Raiht'vi."

"Female Zorahn do not mark themselves," he replies. "The men though, what color were their markings?"

His tone is too casual. "Are you trying to wheedle information out of me?" I ask bluntly. "Why don't you try asking me directly instead?"

His chest shakes with laughter, and I feel the grip of his arm around my shoulder tighten. "I don't think I've ever been spoken to in that tone," he says, his voice rueful. "You're right, *aida*. I'm sorry. Zoraht is a planet with a rigid social structure, and the color of the markings have significance. I was trying to understand who was behind your expedition."

Oh. I didn't expect him to apologize. "Beirax's head was tattooed with blue whorls," I reply. "Mannix's were black and brown."

"A scientist and a technician," he replies. "What color were the female's hair shells?"

I try and picture Raiht'vi. "Blue, I think. Her clothes were white."

"Highborn too," he says tightly. "If her shells were blue, she's a scientist as well."

The suppressed anger in his voice is hard to miss. "You don't like the scientists?" I'm doing the same thing I accused Arax of; I'm wheedling information out of him.

"No," he admits, closing his eyes. "It's an old wound. When we were exiled, we weren't allowed to say goodbye to our families. One moment, our lives were normal. The next, we were held in cages, awaiting transport to the prison planet."

Oh, wow. That sounds... awful.

"The exile is necessary," he says. "The scientists are probably right to be cautious. But the way it's done..." His voice trails off, and he's quiet for a long moment. "We don't have tech. We can't communicate with our families back home. We were dropped onto a primitive planet with no food, no supplies. Nothing to ensure our survival. The scientists want us to die, but they don't have the nerve to kill us outright. So, they do this instead." He gestures to the night sky, his expression bitter.

Oh hey, Raiht'vi? I think you forgot to give me some important context.

Of course Raiht'vi's terrified of the Draekons. She's right to be. If I were in Arax's place, and the scientists had treated me the way they treated him, I would want to kill her.

Because of the scientist's warnings, I've screwed up. I've been lying to Arax and Nyx almost from the first moment. I've let them believe the others are dead. I've told them I'm alone.

Arax's hand closes over mine, and I realize, with a blush, that I'm still touching his muscled arms. They're warm and smooth, silk over steel. "To answer your earlier question," he says, "These tattoos are from the testing. Zorahn men are tested yearly for the Draekon mutation."

"And they found it in you." I stroke his skin, counting the black bands. There are nineteen of them. *Woman up, Vi. Tell them the truth and bear the consequences.* "How old were you when you tested positive?"

"Twenty."

"And the Zorahn exiled you here."

Something else clicks in place. Right before Beirax crashed the ship, he said something about humans serving as seed for the Draekon race. His comment hadn't meant anything to me at that time, but it does now.

Sometime in the distant past, the Zorahn scientists used human genetic material to create the Draekons. *That's the only explanation that makes sense.* That's why Arax and Nyx recognize me, a human, as their mate. That's why the Zorahn came back to Earth for new lab rats. That's probably even why the Zorahn scientists had a cure for leukemia in their back pocket—they've already studied our genetic matter.

The thoughts swirl in my head in a confused, tangled

mess. What the Zorahn did to Arax and Nyx is horrible and cruel. Being exiled to a prison planet because of something you were born with seems vicious and vile.

The human women will restore the Draekons to the glory that's their birthright. Those were Beirax's words. He wants to breed us, mate us to the Draekons. That's why he crashed the ship on this world.

A frisson of anger trickles down my spine. Beirax didn't ask us for permission. He didn't care for our consent. To him, we're no better than animals.

If it were up to me, I'd sleep with them.

I don't know where that thought comes from, but it's true. Even now, I'm leaning against Arax's chest, touching him, my pussy aching with heat at the thought of the two of them taking me and claiming me as theirs.

But I can't. If Beirax's theory is right, then sex with Arax and Nyx will get me pregnant. And then what? I'm supposed to go back to Earth in six months. What would happen if I show up pregnant with a half-dragon baby in my womb? I have no illusions; Uncle Sam would lock me up in the equivalent of Area 51 faster than I can blink.

Arax's arms suddenly feel like bands of steel. I start to struggle, and he frees me instantly. "Are you alright, Viola Lewis?"

"Tell me why you said you wish I hadn't overheard you." I twist around and look into his eyes. "Because you will take me by force, and you prefer that I live in ignorance of that fact?"

His face goes carefully blank. "I don't know what will happen," he says. "To the best of my knowledge, no one has transformed into a Draekon for a thousand years. The ThoughtVaults are incomplete. What you overheard was a speculation."

His hands clench into fists at his side. "I am a man as well as a beast, Viola Lewis." There's an edge of pain in his voice, and I want to wrap my arms around him and comfort him. It bothers me to see his distress. "I gave you my word earlier that you will be safe. Even from me."

It doesn't look good for the *'don't sleep with the hot alien dragons'* plan because when he promises to keep me safe, I believe him. Even though I have no logical reason to.

I'm about to open my mouth and tell him that I trust him. I'm about to tell him everything.

Then I see it on the horizon.

Three rockets of light shoot up from the direction where I left the space ship. One white flare, followed by a red one, and then a white one again.

A grim expression fills Arax's face. "That's a Zorahn flare," he says, his voice utterly cold. "Tell me again, Viola Lewis, how many of you survived the crash?"

I'm in deep trouble.

12

NYX

Our mate lied to us to protect her fellow humans. Her logic is deeply misguided. The ship has crashed in the lowlands and will get swept away in the floods that are almost upon us. Even without the threat of the rainy season, the human women will need our help to survive on this world.

I don't understand what she hopes to gain by keeping them a secret, but one thing is certain. I can't fault Viola Lewis' heart. She means well.

"They're in mortal danger?" Her voice rises in panic as she paces at the mouth of the cave. "We have to go to them. What was I thinking? Harper was injured, damn it. I should have never left them alone."

Arax and I exchange uneasy looks. "What happened to the human?" This is a dangerous world. A woman the size of our mate will not be able to protect herself. The dwals are vicious during the day. At night, the hairus swarm the air.

"Harper brushed against some kind of fungus. An orange one."

Bast. "Growing on the bark of a tree?" I demand.

"Yes," she says nervously. "Why?"

"Because it's very poisonous," Arax replies, his expression grim. "Rorix brushed against it. He went into a coma for three months."

"Rorix is Draekon? What could possibly hurt one of you?" She pivots to us, a stricken look on her face. "Sofia and Ryanna were going to help her back to the ship and put her in stasis, but if she became a dead weight..." She shivers at the thought. "What if they're still outside? What if they can't find shelter? I have to go to them."

When our mate looks at me the way she is right now, I want to give her everything, but it's impossible. "It's too dangerous, *aida*," I tell her regretfully. "This close to the rainy season, the hairus swarms are thick in the air, each one half as big as this cave. They will swoop down from the sky, and they'll feed on anything that moves."

I pull her into my arms and breathe in the scent of her. She smells of worry and panic, but underneath the fear, there's a distinct note of arousal. My body reacts to her heat and her nearness, and my cock hardens. "It will be dawn in an hour." I stroke her back soothingly, and she wraps her hands around my neck. "As soon as the sun's first rays touch the ground, we will set off to find your friends."

This close to her, it's hard to ignore my own need. I want to fling her down on the floor of this cave and take her, deep and hard. I want to hear her soft cries of passion, feel her nails rake down my back.

The urge to mate presses down on me like a physical weight.

Then I feel her fingers caress my erect cock through my loincloth. "I'm your mate, isn't that right?" she asks us. She tugs her shirt with its strange fastenings free, and her pale, voluptuous breasts are exposed to the night air, with their pink-tipped rosy-hued nipples. "Then take me."

The beast roars its approval in my brain. She welcomes the mating bond, it crows triumphantly. She will be ours now.

And when we are mated, the beast will be free.

13

VIOLA

L et's be honest. It's not going to be a hardship to sleep with them.

My motives aren't entirely pure, okay? I didn't know the ship had flares, and neither did any of the other women. The call for help could have only come from one of the Zorahn.

And the color code? We might not have learned about the rigid class structure on Zoraht, and we definitely didn't learn how to survive if your ship crashes on the wrong planet, or what to do if you ran into hunky exiled prisoners who turn into dragons. But the one thing the Zorahn taught us was how to yell for help. *The sequence of 'white, red, and white' is the Zorahn code for mortal danger.*

If Raiht'vi or Beirax are afraid, then it really doesn't bode well for the eight women on the ship.

I don't care about the Zorahn. I just care about my girls. Harper, Sofia, and Ryanna are out there somewhere. Olivia and May are hurt. The others are hopefully still in stasis, but I can't be sure they're safe either.

Birds the size of cars swooping down on anyone who

moves? Stupid jackal things as big as a horse hanging around waiting to attack anyone who seeks water? This world is crazy.

The only creatures more powerful than the birds and the jackals, fine, the hairus and the dwals, are Arax and Nyx, because *they can change into dragons.*

And the only thing stopping Arax and Nyx from changing into these Draekons right this second? We haven't had sex.

Houston, we have a solution.

I swallow hard as I place my hand on Nyx's cock. The dark haired Draekon studies me with hooded eyes. "What are you doing, Viola Lewis?"

Arax looks at me with serious eyes. "You need rest, sweet one."

Their response isn't encouraging. I pull my hand away from Nyx's cock, abashed. Maybe going straight for the goods is a little too forward.

You've never had anal sex before, Vi. They're huge. Are you really ready for this?

I lay my hand on Nyx's chest. "I just want to touch you," I murmur. "I've never seen skin like this before." It's the truth. I inhale his spicy scent and stroke the bronze skin. There's a faint pattern of scales under the tattoos. Is it new? I don't remember seeing it earlier.

Nyx inhales sharply as my fingers caress his body, but he doesn't stop me.

Something about this planet makes me so horny. Or maybe it's the hotties running around wearing next to nothing. Draekons would make great male strippers. *Just sayin'.*

"When did you get these piercings?" I toy with the barbell through Nyx's right nipple.

He catches my hand. "Careful, *aida*. You play with fire."

His warning doesn't deter me. I slide my hand down his chiseled muscles, tracing the beautiful V leading right to his groin. I've almost forgotten my plan. My body trembles and my sex aches. I may have an ulterior motive, but I want this as much as they do.

Arax watches as I touch Nyx, and the heat in his eyes encourages me. My hand brushes Nyx's cock again, and this time, he reciprocates, slipping a hand down my pants to cup my pussy.

I'm soaking wet, and now he knows it.

His fingers swirl over my lower lips, parting them and sliding inside the wet heat.

"You didn't answer my question," I murmur while I'm still capable of coherent thought.

"On our home world, we get piercings when we come of age. To show we are sexually available."

"Mmm." I stroke up Nyx's length, feeling the soft skin slide over the steel of his cock. Looking at Arax, I lick my lips, openly inviting him to join in, but the other male doesn't take the bait. Feeling deliberately wicked, I push them.

"Really? Mannix and Beirax didn't have piercings," I say innocently. "At least, I didn't see any."

At the mention of the Zorahn men, Nyx half purrs, half growls. The sound vibrates through me, increasing my arousal.

Arax's gaze narrows, and when he responds, his voice is silky. "If you can think of other men while we pleasure you, Viola Lewis," he says, "perhaps we should work harder at distracting you."

Nyx plunges two fingers into my pussy, revenge and humor glinting in his eyes. His thumb glides over my clitoris.

"Ah..." My body tightens.

"Are you close to peaking?"

"Yes," I admit, breathless with lust.

He removes his fingers, the scaly bronzed bastard. "This time, I wish you to peak with me," he says.

Nyx's cock throbs in my grip. I explore every ridge, every vein and throbbing inch of his member, spreading the precum all over him like lube until he's thick and shiny, and absolutely mouthwatering.

He groans, his head thrown back, his face a mask of pleasure.

His obvious desire encourages me. I lean forward and put my mouth over his nipple. He sucks in a breath as I circle his piercing with my tongue.

"Do you like it?" Nyx asks, his voice hoarse.

"Hmmm?"

"Do you like the piercing?"

Oh yeah. Very much. Already massive, his cock grows hard and thick as I tease his nipple. I ache to taste Nyx. My mouth is watering—I've never been so excited to go down on a guy in my life. But when I start to sink to my knees, Nyx stops me. "Wait. Do not forget. You have two mates."

How can I forget? The idea of sucking Nyx while Arax watches is making me quiver. But Nyx is right. It would be a lot more fun if the big Draekon joined us.

"Please?" I turn to Arax, openly flaunting my naked breasts at him, a little surprised that I would act this brazen. Like there's a wanton sex goddess inside me, and all it took was a quick trip to another planet to let her out. "Join us."

His face is torn. I sense reluctance in him, but there's need as well. "I want to make sure you are well, Viola Lewis."

"I'm fine, I promise."

He takes a step toward me. Leaning forward, I take his cock in my free hand. "Never better." I repeat the lubing and pumping action on him, reveling in the expression of naked desire on my dragon lover's face.

Nyx's hand plays between my parted legs. Arax wraps his hand around my neck and pulls me toward him. He kisses me deeply, passionately, and I'm lost in his touch. He's a good kisser.

I almost forget what I'm doing, but Nyx pinches my nipple.

"Hey," I gasp.

"You liked it." Nyx shows me his wet fingers and keeps fondling my pussy as I stroke both of them off. My palms heat up. A tingling feeling spreads through my fingers, everywhere the precum touches.

My thighs clench as Nyx rubs me just in the right spot. "I'm close," I whimper. I've never orgasmed so easily or quickly in my life.

"Good." The men take their own cocks in hand, and stroke faster.

"Wait," I say, remembering my plan. "Shouldn't...I mean, I want you inside me."

Arax's expression is knowing. "Do you really, Viola Lewis?" he asks. "Or are you doing this so we can become Draekons at will?"

I bite my lip, flushing with shame at how easily he's read through me. "I want that," I admit, unwilling to lie to them. "But I also want you."

"Are you are sure of that?" Nyx asks. He's let go of his cock and watches me closely. He doesn't look disappointed, but I feel horrible.

"I want you," I tell them both. "I don't know why, but I felt connected to you from the moment I saw you." I raise my hands in defense, wishing I hadn't tried to manipulate these men. "Ever since I got here, I've been scared and helpless, and you take that all away. I'm just afraid—" My voice chokes off. I'm so afraid. I'm supposed to be the brave one, climbing on a spaceship to explore worlds beyond, going into the jungle to save everyone, doing everything I can to make things right.

Who am I kidding? I did everything I could to save my dad, and he still died.

"Oh, *aida*," Nyx croons, folding me in his arms. His smoky scent is more comforting than ever.

"I'm fine," I protest, blinking against tears. I will not cry. *I will not cry.* I run my hands over Nyx's skin. He's warm and smooth and strong, and touching him helps a lot. I sag into him. "I just need this." *This* being a screaming orgasm, my body impaled on two cocks. I can't bring back my dad or put the Zorahn ship back together, but I'm hornier than I've ever been in my life, and at least I can do something about it.

"Come here, Viola Lewis," Arax says. He puts his finger under my chin and tips it up, looking into my eyes. "You want this?" he asks once again.

"Yes," I whisper. The set of his mouth is so stern. I trace the worry lines there, and he catches my finger in his mouth, nipping playfully.

A smile lights up his face. "Very well," he concedes.

Nyx wraps his arms around my waist, the hard length of his cock pressing into my bottom. "We need you, Viola Lewis," he says, his breath tickling my ear. "We will go slowly."

"I don't mean to rush you—"

"No." Arax puts a finger over my lips. "We wished to mate the moment we saw you. It is best for all that we claim you now when we are in control."

Right. The dragons. I gulp.

Arax kisses me again. He positions me so that he's lying on the ground and I'm straddling him. Suddenly, I can think of nothing other than the feel of his erect cock sliding along my backside.

"We are ready when you are. Put my cock inside you."

I kneel up and move over his shining member. At least the fluid will ease my way.

"Slowly," Nyx murmurs at my back, steadying me as I sink onto Arax's waiting rod. There's a slight burn as my folds give way to his thick girth, but arousal pours through me, slickening my pussy further, drenching his bronze skin. I slide all the way onto him. My womb cramps once, and then he's seated deep inside me.

"*Aida,*" Arax breathes, closing his eyes, his face contorting with raw desire.

I know exactly how he feels.

I'm panting with need, letting him fill every inch of my body and my mind. I can't even contemplate moving. Arax remains still inside me, and for that, I'm grateful. One thrust and I might shatter, and I want to savor this moment forever.

Heat stirs deep inside me, and I realize that as perfect as his cock is, the thick precum has an added benefit. The fluid warms me.

Arax lifts his hips, pushing a little deeper.

"Oh God. Oh fuck." I whimper. My body tingles as he pumps into me, taking a slow and tortuous rhythm.

Arax catches my hand and kisses my fingertips. The unexpectedly tender gesture causes a lump to form in my throat. My pussy clenches on him, hard.

He cups my breasts reverently, and I return the favor, brushing my thumbs over his nipple piercings. Arax's thrusts grow urgent, but then he stops.

Nyx kisses the back of my neck. "My turn."

"Oh God. I don't think—"

"Trust your mates," Nyx says. He presses another kiss on my skin, and he bends me forward. I lay flush on Arax's broad chest, my fingers dimpling his skin as Nyx prepares my bottom for his assault.

He takes his sweet time, oiling up his fingers and probing me. I wriggle my bottom a little, and he smacks it.

"Stop that," I say even as Arax orders, "Do that again."

Nyx spanks then squeezes my bottom, and my inner muscles tighten on Arax's cock. I don't know if I should protest the spanking or beg for another, but before I make up my mind, Arax shakes his head.

"She gushes when you do that," he says. "It's too much. Hurry, Nyx. I'm close."

Something large and warm touches my back hole, and instinctively, I tense.

"Hush, sweet one." Nyx's large hands knead the back of my neck. "You are safe with us."

He pushes in. I inhale sharply as he enters my ass, and my fingers tighten their grip on Arax's biceps as my ring stretches to accommodate his thickness. Hearing my gasp, he stops moving until I relax, then he pushes forward again, boldly going where no man has gone before.

I chuckle at my pun, and Arax raises an eyebrow. "What?" he asks.

"Nothing." I angle my head and kiss him. Our dueling tongues distract me from Nyx's plundering of my last virginity. They both push deep in my body, filling me beyond what I thought possible.

The next thing I know, the two men are moving, rocking me between them. Arax's muscles flex under my hands, and he never takes his eyes off me.

Nyx pushes forward, Arax presses up, and I dance between them, my nipples tight, brushing against Arax's heated skin. I lick his shoulder, and a needy sound escapes his throat.

A pulse of heat shoots through me at his male groan.

Nyx's teeth graze my shoulder. His thrusts grow more forceful. I cry out, loving the way the two of them feel. The friction of two cocks inside me sets off every nerve ending in both my pussy and ass, and pleasure begins to burn my brain.

"We peak together," Arax commands.

I don't care that he's so bossy. I just don't want the movement to stop.

My moans get louder. The men speed up, keeping their rhythm. I teeter on the knife edge of orgasm, filled to the brim with feeling. My head shakes back and forth, but it's too late to stop the explosion. I hurtle helplessly towards pleasure, and when it hits, I may shatter.

Nyx slams into me and Arax's cock plunges deeper. White hot pleasure blinds me. I shout as my climax overtakes me, and through the cloud of lust in my mind, I hear them shout too as they find their releases. My pussy and ass spasm, milking them as they pump their cum into my willing holes.

I am undone.

The strong arms of my men hold me together.

I fall asleep thinking that the Draekons may be onto something. Two cocks are better than one.

WHEN AWARENESS RETURNS, I feel a stirring of fear. Nyx and Arax aren't Draekons. The two of them lie on either side of me, and they are definitely men.

"You haven't changed," I say, sitting up in alarm, reaching for my top to cover my breasts, though I'm fairly sure it's a little too late for modesty. "Why haven't you transformed?"

Has there been a mistake? Are they wrong about me being their mate, and if so, why does that thought bother me so much?

Nyx shrugs. "At the moment, I find myself quite unconcerned." He tugs my top out of my hands, and he strokes my nipples, watching them harden at his touch. "I have much more interesting things on my mind."

Arax gives me a thoughtful look. Is it my imagination, or is he keeping something from me? "Remember, Viola Lewis," he says, "No one from Zoraht has shifted to Draekon in living memory. It's quite possible that the records in the ThoughtVaults are incomplete."

A ray of light illuminates the cave. "It's dawn," he continues. "The sun will rise shortly, and we can leave to find your friends."

He's right. I jump to my feet, wincing as I feel the ache between my legs. It's going to hurt to walk today, but it was well worth it. When I think back on the way Arax and Nyx slid into me, a shiver wracks my body.

I dress quickly and run my fingers through my hair, before tying it back with a hairband that serves as a reminder of Earth. *You'll be back soon,* I tell myself, ignoring the pang I feel at the thought of leaving my two Draekons. *In a year, this is all going to seem like a distant memory.*

As I get ready, my thoughts are torn. My chest is tight with worry for the other women, but there's a small hard knot of pain underneath.

Meeting Arax and Nyx is the best thing that's happened to me in a long time.

And I'm going to have to let them go.

14

ARAX

She is our mate. The dragon inside me purrs with contentment at the memory of her sweet body, her breathy cries, her soft whimpers.

Not just the dragon.

Had I not been exiled, I would have been bonded within a season. I was the Firstborn of Zoraht, and my bonding would have been based on political considerations. I wouldn't have been able to choose for myself.

For the first time in my life, I see the exile as a blessing, not a curse. Viola Lewis is a revelation. She is small but strong-willed. She is unconcerned with power; her thoughts are to protect her companions. When she smiles at me, my heart stutters in my chest, and when she leans against me, I want to wrap my arms around her and cherish her.

The cave we've taken refuge in is only a few lengths above ground. The two of us carried her up, and we're prepared to carry her down, but she waves off our help. "I used to climb when I was younger," she says. "My father called me his little goat. I can manage."

I keep a careful eye on her, but she's right. She can climb

the cliffs without our help. "Which way is the ship?" I ask when we reach the ground. The flares came from the lowlands to the west of the Na'Lung cliffs, but that's a large area, and we need to make speed.

I worry about what we're going to find when we get there. For my mate's sake, I hope her companions have survived.

Viola Lewis looks around, her dark eyes confused. "I don't know," she says. "Everything looks the same to me. Can you take me back to the spot where the Dwals attacked me? I think I can retrace my steps from there."

"Of course."

We set out. I lead the way, and Nyx brings up the rear, our mate sandwiched protectively in between. If anything attacks, it will have to go through Nyx and me to get to her, and that won't be easy.

I set a brisk pace, and we don't journey long before our mate is breathing hard, struggling to keep up. As soon as I realize that, I come to a dead stop. "I'm sorry, *aida*," I tell her. "I wasn't thinking. I will carry you."

"I'm fine," she says through gritted teeth. "I run marathons. I'll keep up."

The translator tells me that a marathon is a race in which humans line up and run for no reason at all. Not to catch prey, not to escape a predator. They just run for fun. What a strange world this Earth is.

"Your legs are shorter than ours," Nyx points out patiently. "And you need to acclimatize to this world. The air is thick with moisture, and it makes it difficult to breathe. When we got here, the heat overwhelmed us. There's no shame in asking for help, sweet one."

"Fine," she concedes. "But I'm heavy."

I hoist her on my back, and she wraps her arms around

my neck, and her feet around my hips. "You're as light as a *hairus* feather, Viola Lewis," I tell her. Nyx is much better than I am at getting our mate to agree with him. *Because he appeals to her logic and doesn't order her around,* the creature inside says bluntly.

Ruefully, I admit the truth of that. As Firstborn, I'm used to barking out orders and expecting them to be obeyed. Even in the exile camp, though I'm not Firstborn any longer, Zoraht traditions are ingrained deep into everyone, and with that comes an instinctive deferral to my wishes.

Our mate is from an alien world. She treats me like a regular person.

As does Nyx. The two of them are the only people on this planet to see me as someone other than the Firstborn of Zoraht.

With Viola Lewis on my back, we make much better time, and it isn't long before we're back on the banks of the river. The charred remains of the Dwals are still there.

"We burned them so thoroughly that there isn't enough flesh for scavengers," Nyx points out, his voice chagrined.

Viola puts her arm around his waist. "You did it to protect me," she says. She points to a spot where the grass shows signs of disturbance. "The ship was in that direction."

I exchange a troubled glance with Nyx. I know from our mate's story that she was alone when she stumbled upon the river, but the grass is well-trampled.

More than one person has been along this path.

15

VIOLA

A rax and Nyx set a blistering pace. Two hours later, we're at the ship.

At first glance, *Fehrat 1* looks exactly as we left it. For a split-second, hope stirs in my chest. Could the flares have been an accident?

Then I notice that the mattresses that covered the hole in the ship are gone. They're scattered around the gleaming metal body, and there are giant rips in them as if a creature with sharp claws has torn them to shreds.

Nyx picks up a gleaming obsidian scale from the ground and hands it to Arax without a word. Arax looks at it for a long time, but he doesn't comment.

He doesn't need to say anything. I'm not an idiot. *I'm looking at a Draekon scale.*

My heart pounding, I move toward the opening, but both men stop me. "I'll go first," Arax says, his hands tightening on the throwing knives he wears in a belt slung around his hips. "Nyx, if something happens, don't wait for me. Get Viola Lewis back to the safety of the camp. The rains are almost on us."

Nyx nods grimly. I watch, my throat tight with fear, as Arax climbs up the side of the ship. He looks through the hole, then bites off a curse. "It's clear," he calls to us, dropping into the void.

We're right on his heels. Nyx hoists me up the ship, and I scramble inside, almost gagging from the smell of rotting flesh that assails my nostrils as soon as I step inside.

The ship was in bad shape already because of the crash. But that's nothing compared to the condition it is in now. Panels are torn, instruments destroyed and worst of all, the doors of the stasis chambers hang open, all except one.

Raiht'vi is slumped against the wall, next to Janet's dead body, a weapon in her lap. The heat and the humidity have not been kind to the corpse. That's what I smelt, I realize. Janet's body.

At our movement, the Zorahn woman's eyes open. When she sees Arax and Nyx, her eyes widen with panic, and her grip tightens on the weapon. "Draekon," she hisses. "You took the Earth women already. Have you come back to kill me?"

I watch in horror as she aims the weapon at Nyx, but she's too weak. She slumps forward, and the gun clatters onto the floor. Nyx kicks it out of reach. "She's badly wounded," he says, bending down.

He's right. There's no recognition in her eyes when she looks at me. She'd been unconscious when we'd tried to move her; she'd woken up to warn us, and then she fainted. If she remembers the warning, she's giving no sign of it.

Arax, who put his big body in front of me the instant Raiht'vi opened her eyes, crouches next to the woman. "Open your eyes," he says, a note of cold command threaded through his voice. "Do you know who I am?"

Mannix and Beirax had addressed Raiht'vi deferentially.

Not so Arax. There is arrogance in his tone, and neither Nyx nor Raiht'vi seems to think it's out of place.

Raiht'vi nods weakly. "Arax," she says, answering him as if by instinct. "I saw you in the Royal Assembly once."

Royal Assembly? I get the sense I'm missing something.

"Tell me what happened here," Arax says to the Zorahn woman.

"My stasis pod was opened by two Draekons," Raiht'vi mutters, her voice faint. "Some of the other pods were already open, and four Earth women were awake."

"Which four?" Could Harper, Sofia, and Ryanna be among them? Guilt sloshes my insides when I think of the three women who set off with me to find food and water. *Please let them have made their way back to the ship.*

"The Earth women's names are not my concern," Raiht'vi snaps, with a flash of her former spirit.

You fucking bitch, I will cut you.

Arax gives her a cold look and her defiance wilts. "Paige Watkins, Felicity Rollins, May Archer and Bryce MacFarland," she replies. "As I watched, the two Draekon opened another pod, and they pulled out the red-haired woman."

"Olivia," I say out loud. She was the only redhead on the ship. "She had a broken leg?"

Raiht'vi seems to wage an internal war about whether to acknowledge my question, and she nods curtly. "As soon as the men sighted the woman, they began to change."

Nyx looks startled. "They shifted to Draekon?"

I remember what Arax told me. Men with the Draekon mutation transform when they see their mates for the first time. It seems that the two mystery men, whoever they are, think that Olivia is their mate.

The Zorahn woman acts as if she doesn't hear Nyx. I have no idea why, but the two men do. Nyx's lips tighten, and Arax looks furious. "You will answer his questions as if they were mine," he grits out.

Raiht'vi's eyes flash with anger, but her voice is compliant. "Your will, Firstborn."

Firstborn? Earlier, Arax was able to guess at Raiht'vi's occupation and status from the color of her garments and the shells she wore in her hair. Now, Raiht'vi doesn't deign to acknowledge Nyx's existence, but she obeys Arax even though it's clear she doesn't want to.

Zoraht must have a rigid caste system. And just as obviously, Arax is a very big deal.

Later, Vi. Focus on what's important. The missing women.

"If they shifted to Draekon, why is the ship still intact?" I ask Raiht'vi. "They should have torn it apart when they transformed."

"The beasts had the presence of mind to jump outside," she replies sourly. "The Draekon took the women. I tried to stop them, but I was too weak to fight."

Arax gives the weapon that Raiht'vi was holding a dismissive glance. "You can't hurt a Draekon with that." He strides over to the only unopened pod and pulls the door open.

As I expect, it's Beirax. Arax sucks in his breath when he takes in the Zorahn's extensive injuries. When Raiht'vi notices, her teeth bare into a snarl. "The traitor deserves to die for what he did," she says fiercely. "Because of him, I will rot on this planet for the rest of my days."

A cold trickle runs down my spine. "What do you mean, you'll rot on this planet for the rest of your days?" I demand. "The High Emperor will send a ship to rescue us, won't he? He personally guaranteed our safety."

She laughs bitterly. "This is the prison planet, foolish human," she sneers. "There is no escape. No Zorahn pilot can navigate the asteroid belt that surrounds this world. Look at the damage we sustained." She shakes her head. "The High Emperor will pay damages to your people for the actions of the traitor Beirax. As for us?" Her gaze falls to the floor, and her voice trails off into a whisper. "We will die on this planet."

16

NYX

The stunned expression on her face makes it clear —*she didn't know.* Our mate thought she could escape from this world.

Arax and I help the Highborn woman back to the stasis pod. Her face is a frozen mask of pain; blue blood trickles from a cut on her forehead. She allows me to touch her, which leads me to believe she's more injured than she appears to be. Under normal circumstances, no Highborn woman would allow a Lowborn thief anywhere near her.

"What do we do now?" Viola Lewis asks us, her voice disconsolate, once the three of us are alone. "Should we go looking for the Draekons who took Olivia and the others? Should we try and find Harper, Ryanna, and Sofia?" She sinks to the floor, then recoils in distaste as a burst of wind brings another whiff of the dead woman's odor.

I don't like the feel of that wind. If the skies open when we are trapped in the lowlands, we will drown.

"Let's bury the dead while we figure that out," I say. The Zorahn technician must be laid to rest, as must the dead Earth woman, lest the smell attracts the Dwals. The technician and the Earth woman, deserve better than to have their corpse torn to shreds by the predators. "We can't leave them like this, *aida*."

"You're right." Tears swim in her eyes, and she wipes them away with the back of her hand. "Poor Janet. This is not the adventure she intended."

Arax and I lift the bodies outside, and the smell almost makes me retch. Ever since I shifted, my senses seem keener. Maybe this is part of being Draekon.

We wrap the dead in the broad, triangular leaves of a *langobar* plant. Arax and I dig a pair of crude graves, using our throwing knives to break the ground. The soil is tightly packed, and the digging goes slowly. The sun is high in the sky by the time we are ready to lower the woman's body into the ground. "Is it the custom of your people to sing to the dead?" I ask our mate.

She shakes her head. "We make speeches," she says quietly. "We remember what we loved about them." The tears fall freely, and her shoulders shake as she sobs. Instantly, we're at her side. I'm cursing myself for my thoughtlessness.

Some mate I'm turning out to be.

17

VIOLA

I'm not crying because of Janet. I'm not even crying because I appear to be stuck on this stupid, too-hot, too-filled-with-toxic-plants, no-chocolate-in-sight planet.

No, the tears that pour down my cheeks are because this crude burial on this jungle world brings forth memories of my dad. Growing up, it was always the two of us. We were a team. Now, I'm all alone.

Nyx wraps an arm around me. "Viola Lewis," he says, his voice distressed. "I'm sorry. I know Raiht'vi's words were a shock. Please don't cry."

"That's not why," I sniff, leaning against Nyx's welcoming shoulder, really liking the way his hand strokes my arm. "I haven't even thought about *that* yet."

"Then what is it, sweet one?" Arax crouches next to me, his eyes boring into mine. "What upsets you? What can we do to help?"

Their concern is *nice*. They're both so worried for me, and it feels really comforting to know that they care that I'm upset.

"My father died recently." I wipe my eyes on my sleeve. My top is starting to look quite ragged. I guess it wasn't built for a spaceship crash, being attacked by predators, and everything else that's happened to me since I arrived on this planet. "I'm still processing his loss."

"I can relate," Arax says, an understanding expression on his face.

Of course they can. They were exiled to an alien world because they tested positive for the Draekon mutation. They had to leave friends and family behind; they weren't even allowed to say good-bye. They know loss, intimately and well.

We hold each other, and for a space of time, I don't feel alone.

Arax and Nyx lower Janet's leaf-wrapped body into the narrow grave. Nyx pulls out his knife and slices a cut in his palm. I gasp, but he doesn't seem to register the pain. He lets the blood drop down on the poor school teacher's body. "Night to night," he says quietly. "Earth to earth. Blood to ashes. May your light find a home in the darkness."

I watch him, fascinated. This must be a Zorahn ritual, because Arax follows, cutting himself as well. "Journey safely into the void, friend of our mate."

Then it's my turn. I approach the grave. "I didn't know you very well, Janet." I stare at the leaf-covered body. "But you always had a kind word for everyone." I take a deep breath and step back, and Arax and Nyx fill the grave with soil. I stand back and watch, oddly consoled that we're having a funeral for the high school teacher. *It feels cleansing.*

They bury Mannix next. "What now?" I ask them after a few moments of quiet reflection. "Which set of women do we go after?"

"The ones that are alone," Arax replies decisively. "The

others are with Draekons. They will not be hurt. But the unaccompanied women are in danger in this world."

"The Draekons that took Olivia and the others," I ask him hesitantly, almost afraid to hear his reply, "Are they friends of yours? Do you know who they are?"

He shakes his head, but his expression is uncertain. "I don't think it's our exile batch," he says. "It's time to move the camp to higher ground. Everyone is busy hunting for food and laying stores for the rainy season."

"Your exile batch?"

"We were the fifth."

Nyx looks up with a peculiar expression on his face. "You think it was another exile batch?" he asks. "Could another set of Draekons be only a few days away from us?"

"We don't have time to look," Arax replies at once. "The rains are almost here."

Nyx nods reluctantly. "You're right. Let's go after the three women who are alone."

"What about Raiht'vi and Beirax?" I don't like either of the Zorahn very much, but we can't leave them in the stasis pods. They're injured. Defenseless. "Should we leave them alone?"

"We can't take them with us." Arax's voice is regretful. "They're too badly hurt. Especially the man." He cups my chin with his hands and looks into my eyes. "We will come back for them."

His hands are rough and calloused, and when he touches me, a shiver runs through my body. "Okay."

"They will be safe enough," Nyx reassures me. "The Dwals cannot open the stasis pods, and the Draekon aren't interested in Zorahn." He extends his arm to me. "Viola Lewis, let me carry you."

A giggle breaks out. I've slept with the two men. Each of

them has carried me on their back. Whenever they call me Viola Lewis, it feels so strangely formal. "My friends call me Viola. Or Vi."

Nyx winks. "What do your mates call you?"

I blush red, and both of them chuckle at me.

I smile at the two aliens. They've fed me. Pleasured me. Comforted me when I cried. Arax is obviously Highborn. He barks out orders and expects them obeyed, but at the same time, he's protective and tender. Nyx seems less intense, easier to smile and laugh, but he too watches out for me.

Maybe being stuck on the prison planet isn't such a bad thing after all.

"You can't carry me around everywhere," I tell Nyx. "Let me walk for a little while."

He gives me a doubtful look. "Please?" I ask again.

To my surprise, it's Arax that nods. "Come on then," he says with a smile. "Let's go find your friends."

18

ARAX

We set off again after a quick meal. The women's trail is easy to follow, and we make good time. Viola keeps up without too much difficulty, which startles me. "Do you need rest?" I ask her after we've been walking for a distance.

Her face is shiny with perspiration, and her hair sticks to her head, but she shakes her head. "I feel fine," she says. "I haven't run in ages, but I guess I'm not as out of shape as I thought."

I study Viola covertly. It might be my imagination, but I'm willing to swear that her body is changing. Her muscles are sleeker and more defined. Her skin seems to glow. Even the injury on her forehead has healed without a trace of a scar.

Her body is getting ready to bear Draekon youngling. That's the only possible explanation for the changes she's undergoing.

Should I tell her?

An innate sense of caution makes me hold my tongue. Viola has received wave after wave of bad news. First, her ship was deliberately crashed on this planet. Then, half her companions were taken, and the three women she set out with to explore this world are missing. They might even be dead. We buried one of her compatriots, and she's just discovered that she's stuck on this world until the end of her days.

I have just comforted her through her tears once today; I have no wish to see her cry again. When we find her friends, when we take her to our cliff homes, then I will tell her everything. And if she's furious with me for hiding the truth from her, then I will accept her anger.

She is my mate, and I will protect her. Even if she hates me for it.

19

VIOLA

I could use some good news.

Strangely, I'm not too worried about Olivia, May, and the others. They're with people. They'll be fed and taken care of. Olivia might be a ditz, but May's tough. Despite her broken arm, she was ready to set off with us to explore this planet. She'll take care of the women.

It's Harper, Sofia, and Ryanna that I'm frantic about. The orange fungus that Harper brushed against sent a Draekon into a three-month coma. Has it killed her or did Sofia's quick thinking with the epinephrine injection save the blonde Californian swim coach? Then there are the pee-in-my-pants-scary Dwals, with their excessively sharp teeth and their penchant for hovering by the water looking for prey. Arax and Nyx needed to transform into Draekons to take them down—what chance do my three friends have against them?

I gave Ryanna Beirax's weapon. All I can hope is that she has enough presence of mind to use it if they're attacked.

Arax walks in front of me; Nyx brings up the rear. The two men stop from time to time to make sure they haven't lost the trail, but otherwise, they don't talk. We've been marching for an hour and a half when Nyx shouts out. "Stop."

He crouches by a plant, his face breaking out into a wide smile. "Look at this," he says, pointing to the strange sky-blue bush.

At first glance, I don't see what catches Nyx's attention. Arax does, and he explains for my benefit. "See that weaving?"

I look more carefully, and I notice what Nyx's sharp eyes spotted. Tucked into the foliage, there's a long strip of grass, woven into a shape that resembles a Celtic knot. "What is it?" I ask them.

Arax looks exultant. "That's Ferix's mark."

"Ferix is from your exile batch?" Dare I hope that my girls are safe?

"Yes," he replies. "When your spaceship crashed, Nyx and I were on a hunt. Rorix and Ferix were out as well, as were Vulrux and Thrax. And it seems Ferix ran into your companions."

Nyx sniffs at the grass weaving. "They're only a half-day ahead of us," he says, standing up. "They're heading to the Na'Lung Cliffs."

"Na'Lung? That's where we were last night in, isn't it? Why are they going there?"

Nyx grins widely. "Because it is our home," he says. "In the dry season, we spend most of our time in the lowlands, but when the plains flood, we live on the cliffs."

When Nyx says home, I think about my tiny apartment. It wasn't much, but I had a couch. A bathroom. Indoor plumbing. But I'm not on Earth anymore. There's no TV in this planet. No Netflix, not even electricity.

I'm hot and sweaty. I'd happily give up my first born

child for a shower, but things like that are in the past. We're on a primitive planet. No technology, as Arax pointed out. Their homes are probably like the cave we took shelter in last night.

Arax sees my face fall. "What's the matter, *aida*?" he asks. "I thought you'd be relieved that your companions have been found."

I feel like a complete, total jerk. They've saved me from predators and fed me. They've crisscrossed the jungle so that I can find my friends. I'm pouting because I have to live in a cave? I need to get my priorities straight. *Harper, Sofia, and Ryanna are safe.* That's the only thing that matters.

I straighten my shoulders. "Everything's fine."

Nyx looks skeptical. Arax is going to probe further—I can tell—but a flash of lightning distracts him. "The rains aren't too far away," he says grimly. "We need to get Viola to safety."

"What about Beirax and Raiht'vi? We can't let them drown."

"You're right," he replies. "Nyx, take Viola home. I'll get the two scientists."

"Whoa," I protest immediately. "No way. You can't manage the two of them by yourself."

Arax's chin lifts up. "You're not coming," he says. "It's not safe."

Nyx nods in agreement. "Arax is right. We're your mates. Our first priority is to protect you, *aida*."

I glare at the two infuriating Draekon. "Stop coddling me," I say crossly. "I can take care of myself."

Arax starts to say something, and then his head tilts to a side. His hand goes to his hip, his fingers tightening around the hilt of his throwing knife. A minute later, I hear crashing through the vegetation, and four men appear.

No, not men. Draekon.

The newcomers are as tall as Arax and Nyx. Their skins are bronze, and their nipples are pierced too. But the resemblance ends there. Two of the Draekon are blond, one has sandy brown hair, and the other is as bald as Beirax.

And interestingly, I'm not in the slightest bit attracted to any of them. The intense desire that swept through my body when I saw Nyx and Arax for the first time doesn't appear. *Not that I really expected it to.*

The tension in Arax and Nyx's bodies drains away, and Arax strides forward to greet the arriving men. "I never thought I'd be happy to see Haldax," Nyx mutters, lingering behind with me.

"Which one is Haldax, and why don't you like him?" I whisper back to Nyx.

"He's like Raiht'vi. Won't address a lowborn directly."

I roll my eyes. "That was ridiculous. Seriously. She's stuck on a prison planet, and she's insulting the people that are going to help her? Not too bright, Raiht'vi."

Nyx gives me a sidelong grin. "Is that why you mated with us, Viola? Because we helped you?"

I blush. "I slept with you because you're hot."

Nyx chuckles. "Come on," he says, taking me by my hand. "Let's go meet the others. They're staring at you, wondering who you are. Let's sate their curiosity."

I'm a little nervous as Nyx tugs me to the other Draekons. He's right; they're discreetly surveying me and as I near them, my footsteps slow.

Arax turns around when I approach, and a smile breaks out on his face. "This is Viola Lewis," he says to the others. "She is our mate, Nyx and mine. Viola, this is Strax, Vaarix, Dennox, and Haldax."

Strax and Vaarix are the blonds. Dennox the brown-haired one, and Haldax is the bald one. I'm going to have one hell of a time remembering their names. "Hello," I mutter. "Good to meet you."

Haldax's eyes widen with shock. "What do you mean, Firstborn?"

"He means," Nyx drawls, a truly wicked gleam in his eye, "that she is Arax's mate, and she is mine. When we saw her for the first time, we both transformed into dragons."

Arax gives Nyx an exasperated look. "Thank you, Nyx," he says pointedly. "It appears that the ThoughtVaults are correct. Draekon bondings are between two Draekons and one mate. But we will discuss that later. What brought you here?"

"We saw the object fall from the sky," Haldax says. "We were going to investigate when we ran into Ferix and Rorix. They had already found the alien women."

"They did?" I jump in. "Which ones? Are they okay? Do you know their names?"

The newly-arrived Draekons give me blank looks, and I realize belatedly that of course they wouldn't be able to understand me. No translator. I really hope the ship has spares.

Arax repeats my question to them in Zor. "The golden-haired one, Harper Boyd, is unconscious," Dennox says. Well, I think it's Dennox. I wouldn't bet money on my ability to name the Draekon. "The other two, Sofia Menendez and Ryanna Dickson, are shaken, but unhurt. Ferix, Rorix, and Thrax guard them. They sent us back to fetch the two Zorahn on the ship.

"Two injured Zorahn," Nyx says. "You'll need to be careful when you move them."

Haldax gives Nyx a barely-concealed look of contempt.

Arax begins questioning the Draekon about food supplies, and I turn to Nyx. "Doesn't it bother you?"

He shrugs. "It is the Zorahn way," he says. "I'm lowborn. My father was a thief. In the homeworld, I wouldn't be permitted to approach the Firstborn."

I snort. "That's garbage," I say firmly. "A person's worth is measured by what they do and nothing else. And based on that, you're doing pretty damn well."

"You sound like Arax," Nyx says. "When we landed on this world, he forbade us to care about our blood status. Of course, he's the Firstborn, and everyone listened. Still, old habits die hard."

"You keep calling him the Firstborn. What does it mean?"

Nyx raises an eyebrow. "You don't know? Arax's father was High Emperor Dravex. Lenox is his brother. His younger brother."

"Oh." I digest that. "I'm surprised he isn't more bitter about being exiled."

"That's not who Arax is," Nyx replies, shaking his head. "Listen to him now. He's making sure that there's enough food to last us through the rainy season. He's checking to see if Vulrux, who is the healer, knows about your unconscious friend and the injured scientists. Arax was taught to protect and care for his subjects."

"Is that what we are? Subjects?"

Nyx laughs. "You're our mate, *aida*. You're the furthest thing from a subject."

"Am I really?" I voice something that's been nagging at me since last night. "You haven't transformed to Draekon. What if you've got it wrong? What if I'm not your mate after all?"

Nyx wraps an arm around my shoulder. "Enough of this

conversation, Viola," he says firmly. "I transformed into a dragon when I laid eyes on you. Of course you are our mate. The records of the ThoughtVaults are old, and I've always believed that the scientists didn't reveal everything they knew. There's nothing to worry about." He takes my hand and places it on his chest. A faint pulse under my palm tells me this is his heart. Not quite in the same spot as the human organ, but close enough. "I know you are our mate," he says. "I feel it here."

Arax is done with his conversation. The Draekons bob their heads in my direction, then jog off toward the spaceship. "They'll get Beirax and Raiht'vi," he says. "As well as anything they can salvage from the ship. As for us, we head to the cliffs." He takes my hand in his. "You must be anxious to see your friends, *aida*. If you'd like, I can carry you, and we can make better time."

I accept his offer. I tell myself it's because I'm anxious to see Harper, Sofia, and Ryanna, but I know that's not the truth. I just want to feel my mate's arms around me.

NYX

Through an unhappy turn of chance, I'm the only Lowborn in our exile batch. I've told myself many times that this doesn't bother me. I've told myself that it's a blessing that I'm not like Arax, weighed down by duty.

I didn't realize I've been lying to myself until the moment when Arax introduced Viola Lewis to the other Draekons as our mate. Without hesitation, without chagrin or unhappiness.

To Arax, it's a simple statement of fact. To me, it feels like acceptance.

Then there's Viola's staunch defense. *A person's worth is measured by what they do and nothing else,* she'd said, her eyes flashing with irritation. *And based on that, you're doing pretty damn well.*

For the first time, I don't feel like an outsider, wanting to escape this world. For the first time, a deep contentment fills me. I have a mate. I'm happy, and so is the beast inside me.

We get to the same lower cave we were in last night. It's empty, as I expected it to be. The others must have taken advantage of the daylight to climb higher. "We can spend the night here," I suggest. "And go up tomorrow."

Viola looks relieved. "I'm nervous about meeting everyone," she confesses. "It felt like the Draekon we met were staring at me."

"They were," Arax replies. "Does that surprise you? You are our mate. Because of you, we shifted to Draekon, something that hasn't been done for a thousand years. Of course you're going to be the object of attention."

She grimaces. "Thanks. That makes it a lot easier." She settles down on the floor with a sigh. "I would kill for a shower," she mutters.

The translator explains the word *shower*. I've never heard of anything like it, but I know of something that might be almost as good. "Can you climb for a little while longer?"

She nods. "I'm not tired at all. It's really strange. Yesterday, I walked from the ship to the river, and I was wiped."

"Maybe you're getting used to the air in this world."

She looks doubtful. "Maybe. Where are we climbing?"

"To the eastern face," I reply. "There's a stream there."

"Don't the jackal things hang out by the water?" she asks dubiously. "I don't want to be a dwal snack."

Arax's lips twitch. "Relax, sweet one. The Dwals can't climb. You are safe here."

She grins cheerfully. "In that case, lead on."

21

VIOLA

We climb until the rocks grow wet under our feet. Arax and Nyx hover close, hands out to help me in case I slip. I keep my balance and impress myself. My muscles feel loose and strong, and when the path ends, I feel like I could keep climbing.

We break through the foliage and come upon a beautiful mountain pool, deep and still. The water is clear to the bottom.

"Is it safe?" I ask. Small streams flow around the rocks, but I don't see the purple stain that marks the presence of the *kilpei* flower. There's no sign of Dwals either.

"It's safe."

I strip eagerly, peeling off my suit before I think to wear it into the water. The damn thing needs a wash.

Later. Arax and Nyx already have their loincloths off, and I feast my eyes on their ripped abs, their lean thighs, the deep and sexy V of muscle leading to their groins. Their cocks are out and, yes, they are hard.

It's fitting that their skin is bronze, as if an artist decided to sculpt the most perfect dick ever—times two. Their sheer masculine beauty belongs in a museum.

To hide my ridiculous fixation on their manly bits, I race past them and bound into the water. It's cooler than I expected and perfectly refreshing in the tropical heat.

I scrub at my body, wishing I had a washcloth or a loofah. I dunk several times, pulling at my wet tangles with my fingers.

"Why the hurry?" Nyx asks, laughter dancing in his eyes.

"It's cold," I say shortly.

"Mmm." He nips at my shoulder, and my spine goes liquid. "Let us find a way to warm you."

"Do you guys always think about sex?" I ask, as arousal coils in my belly in response to the rigid dick prodding my bottom. The fact that Nyx's cock is hard as granite in cold water is a testament to his desire—or maybe it's a dragon thing.

"You know, when you guys transformed the first time, the air got cold." I fiddle with my hair. "I thought it'd have happened by now." Nyx is a source of warmth in the chilly pool, so I wrap my legs around him too.

Arax wades closer.

"So eager to see us in Draekon form." Nyx bumps his hips against mine. "But right now, I prefer this one." His cock prods me. He pulls me close, twirls and dips me until I laugh. When he straightens us both, his eyes sparkle. "Shall I convince you of this form's advantage?"

He starts to dip me backward again, and I shriek, grabbing his shoulders. "No, no, I'm convinced, I'm convinced." I'm helpless against his sheer brawny strength, so I cheat and slip my hand between us to find his cock. "Right now, I'm very interested in this form." I bite my lip, amazed that I'm so brazen.

"It's very interested in you too, *aida*." Nyx tilts his head and kisses me with clever lips and teasing tongue, an irresistible seduction that makes me melt into his arms. "

Arax still waits nearby. I want to erase the lines of worry on his otherwise young face. He's so serious all the time, as if the weight of the entire planet rests on him. I appreciate his concern, but I'm grateful for Nyx's 'take it as it comes' attitude. The two of them balance each other out.

"We're safe, right?" I ask him.

He nods.

"Good." I cup water in my hands and splash it in his direction. Hey, what can I say? I like to live dangerously.

Nyx laughs as Arax splutters under the full force of my assault. "Did you just splash me?" he asks, incredulous.

"I'll do it again if you don't join us," I threaten him.

"Is that so?" He strides through the water, his powerful body polished perfection, glistening in the sun. He pulls me from Nyx's arms and claims my mouth with all the pent up intensity of a man returning from war to the sweetheart he left behind.

I rock back, hands on his shoulders to steady myself. His hands cup my bottom, preventing me from slipping under the water.

"Oh my God," I say faintly, when his lips finally leave mine. My Draekons know how to kiss.

"Praying again, sweet one?" He transfers his attention to my nipples, licking, sucking, and pinching until I'm faint with desire. I wrap my legs around his waist and tug him as close as I can.

"I need you inside me, right now—"

That's all I have to say. Arax changes direction, cleaving the water towards the edge of the pool. He sits on a large, flat rock with me straddling him. At first, I think he's going to push inside me, but he turns me around so my back is to his front.

"My turn to claim your ass." His finger snakes between my buttocks to rim my back hole.

"And my turn to savor your sweetness," Nyx settles in front of us. "But first, a taste."

I lean back against Arax with my legs on Nyx's shoulders and Nyx's mouth on my pussy. He does a great job warming me up—in more ways than one.

By the time he's done, I am panting, and Arax has stretched my ass using his fingers. I try not to think about how much I love them playing with my behind. It's so wrong, but it feels so right. I'll never admit it to them—and I don't need to. My happy little whimpers tell them all they need to know.

"Now." Nyx lifts me so I'm standing on the rock, and impales me, his cock sliding deep into my pussy. My legs wrap around him. "Hold me tight, *aida,*" he whispers. He kisses me, and I'm distracted by the feel of his tongue exploring my mouth, Arax somehow balances on the rock and pushes his cock into my ass.

My words come out in an incoherent babble, a mixture of 'Oh My God' and a whole slew of cuss words I hope the translator won't pick up.

After a minute, I lose all ability to speak. Two cocks thrust in and out of my lust-filled body, rubbing all the delicious places inside me. I'm reduced to sensation—a cry, a moan, a feeling, an endless arousal that never peaks but rides the heights of climax on and on and on.

My inner muscles flutter, begging for more. The men grunt and slam into me harder, bouncing me between them in a way has me impaled on one cock, then the other. It's violent and beautiful and pushes me past all pleasure into a white-hot world beyond, but I'm never afraid.

Their arms are like iron bands around me, holding me aloft, my feet no longer touching the ground. Then Nyx falls backward, catching himself and me. Arax follows, pushing frantically inside again. We come in a tangle of limbs and cries, while I tuck my head close to Nyx's chest, safe in the eye of the storm, but also a part of it, my orgasm blending with theirs.

At last Arax flops to his back, breathless. Nyx's chest rumbles with a growly purr that vibrates right through me.

"Synchronized fucking," I gasp.

"What?" Arax props himself up on an arm, facing me with a puzzled look on his face.

"You and me and—" I wave at Nyx. "We could win a gold medal in the sex Olympics."

Nyx and Arax exchange curious glances over my head. No doubt the translator is trying to explain the Olympics to them, and judging from their faces, I get the sense that it's not successful. Their confused expressions set me giggling again, and they join the laughter. Our chests shake with deep, soul-cleansing chuckles, and all my worry washes away.

"So it was good?" Nyx asks when he can speak.

"Yes. That was...orgasmic—I mean, obviously," I babble. "Fan-*fucking*-tastic."

Nyx sits up, cradling me in his arms. Even though he's on the ground, and I'm not, I'm covered in dirt, sweat, and their fluids.

"I need a bath." I wrinkle my nose.

"Me too." Arax gets to his feet.

We bathe and fuck, fuck and bathe until my body is made of goo and I'll forever be horny at the mere thought of this mountain pool. Nyx and Arax feed me, and then we lie together. I play with the scale patterns on their arms and chest and trace their tattoos. They point out animals that have come to witness our wild threesome—bright-feathered birds and little jewel colored lizards.

"I wonder what sort of genes were used to make draekons."

"It's anyone's guess, *aida*," Nyx says, shrugging.

Arax gazes at the sky, his expression thoughtful. "There is no mention of Earth in the ThoughtVaults," he says. "Not even in the restricted sections. Yet the scientists sought a cure for whatever ails Zoraht on your planet." He lets out a long sigh. "The scientists conceal much."

A little lizard darts near us, and Arax catches it, quick as a cat, to show me its tiny scales. "But, since I am exiled," he finishes, a grin growing on his face. "The scientists aren't my problem. They're Lenox's."

The sun sinks, and the stars come out. They point out the ones they recognize and others they've named. I wonder if I can see Earth from here. If I can, it's too small to pick out from the endless cluster, a speck of diamond dust in the endless night.

I hug my knees to my chest. "Can we sleep here? Under the stars?"

"If you'd like," Arax answers.

Arax and Nyx fall asleep easily, but I lie awake in the dark. It's slowly sinking in that I can't go back home. No spaceship is going to come to our rescue. This world, this lush rainforest world, with its poisonous fungi and fruit that tastes like pudding, is my home now.

Is that such a bad thing, Vi? There was nothing left on Earth for you.

And here?

Here there are Arax and Nyx, a voice inside me replies. *Your mates.*

I think I'm falling for them. It's absolutely crazy. Back home, if someone had told me that I would have the warm and fuzzies about a guy after two days, I'd have laughed in their faces.

Things are different on this prison planet. From the moment they met me, Nyx and Arax have protected me. They've fed me and taken care of me. They've held me in their arms, and they've made me feel safe and loved.

What did I have to look forward to on Earth? I'd quit my job when my dad got sick so I could take care of him. The government paid us for becoming Zorahn lab rats, but I'd used it to pay for the crippling medical bills. When I go back home, I'll need to find a job to support myself.

And men? I've never been lucky in love. My dad always told me my soulmate was out there, but after the horrors of the online dating scene, I was ready to give up and settle for being single. *I had my dad,* I'd told myself. *It isn't like I'm all alone.*

Then cancer took him away from me.

My home planet has held nothing but disappointment, but can I really give it up ...*forever?*

Things aren't going to be easy here. I've never been a particularly girly-girl, but I still like my creature comforts. This world doesn't have any. Then there are the missing girls— Olivia, Paige, Felicity, Bryce, and May. We aren't even close to figuring out who took them, and from the grimness that covered Arax and Nyx's faces when they saw the Draekon scale, finding them is going to be an impossible task.

It would be easier if they were dragons. Then, they could

fly the skies, and search for the other women from the air. But they still haven't shifted into the beautiful beasts.

Once again, we've had sex, *and nothing.*

Arax appears unworried, as does Nyx. But each time we do it, and they don't transform, my heart clenches, and it's not just because of the others.

I'm starting to fall for them, but what if they're wrong? What if I'm not their mate?

22

VIOLA

The next morning, we climb to the top. It's quite an arduous climb over beautiful white and orange striped rock, but I manage it with relative ease. Arax watches me thoughtfully, and I dismiss it as his usual protectiveness. I'm sure we're both in agreement—I have no desire to tumble down the cliffs.

"How did they manage to carry Harper up?"

Nyx shrugs. "We've done this for sixty seasons, sweet one. We've had a lot of practice carrying things up and down."

Wait, what?

"You've done this for sixty years?" I gape at the two men, my mouth falling open. "How old were you when you came here?"

"Twenty," Arax replies.

Whoa there. I've been sexcapading with a couple of eighty-year-olds. Oh my God, I'm one of those twenty-some-things that shack up with much older sugar daddies. Except, instead of Christian Louboutin shoes and bottles of Cristal, it was vanilla pudding fruit, poison licked from my skin, and some fish.

Intergalactic dating service, indeed.

"What's the matter?" Nyx asks. I've stopped climbing. There's a small ledge, and I sink down on it, still shocked.

Viola Lewis, you're a dirty, dirty girl.

"You're eighty." My voice is strangled. "On Earth, that's really old."

Nyx gives me a look that suggests he has no idea what the problem is.

"Zorahn age differently," Arax says, his voice amused. He's obviously trying not to laugh at me.

I guess he's right. I'm attracted to them; they're attracted to me. If the *'turning into dragons'* part isn't a problem for me, then I guess that this shouldn't be either.

"Yes," I reply wryly, getting back on my feet. "I can see that."

Nyx smirks. "And when we get home," he says, "we can show you that we're not decrepit."

That makes me laugh. Because they might be eighty in Earth years, but the two Draekons are the furthest thing from decrepit. The aching muscles between my legs are an ever-present reminder of that.

Then again, I'm not going to pass up a chance for some more alien loving. "You should do that," I purr.

Lost in banter, I don't realize we've reached our destination. It isn't until Arax says, "We're here," that I look up.

And my mouth drops open.

The Draekons don't live in caves. They don't sleep on the floor. Whatever concerns I had about roughing it are totally misplaced.

In front of me is a clearing the size of two football fields, and in the clearing, are houses. Actual houses. With real walls. And windows, with some kind of fabric stretched over them to cover them.

I think I want to cry from sheer happiness.

A large open-air building is in the center, with a long table running down the middle, and chairs on either side. They're a bit bigger than grandma's Shaker set because they're built to fit Zorahn, but I won't complain. "That's the dining hall," Nyx says.

I'm not listening because my eyes have locked onto the two women that are sitting at the table with eight men. It's Sofia and Ryanna.

My friends are safe.

When they see me, the two women jump up with shrieks. "Holy crap, Viola," Ryanna screams, throwing her arms around me. "I thought you were dead."

Sofia hugs me tight too, her eyes swimming with tears. "I'm so glad you're okay."

I'm ready to bawl my eyes out too. "Harper?" I ask, almost afraid to hear the answer.

Sofia takes a deep breath. "I don't know," she says. "She's alive, but she's in a coma. Vulrux thinks that she'll come out of it, but I've never seen a reaction like that."

"What happened to you?"

Before we can exchange stories, Arax nudges me. Right. I guess it's time for introductions.

Arax takes my right hand, and Nyx grabs my left. Everyone's attention is instantly upon us. Once the chatter dies down, Arax speaks, his voice clear. "This is Viola Lewis. When Nyx and I first laid eyes on her, we shifted into dragons." He pauses for emphasis. "She is our mate."

Whispered conversations break out among the men. On their faces, I see curiosity and naked need. "The legends are true?" one of them asks, wonder in his voice. "We shift into beasts when we sight our mate? That's not a myth?"

"It's not a myth," Nyx answers. A couple of the Draekon do the 'we-can't-hear-the-Lowborn-talk' thing they seem to do so well, but the others acknowledge his words, their eyes widening with awe.

"It is said that once the bonding is complete, the Draekon may shift at will," another man asks. "Is it true, Firstborn?"

A hot flush of shame fills me. I know I'm not being rational, but their failure to transform into dragons feels like my fault.

"Not yet," Arax says calmly. "Our mating bond will take some time. But let there be no doubt," he says, his tone hardening, "Viola Lewis is my mate. Nyx is my pair-bond. They speak with my voice." His eyes lock on the two men that ignored Nyx earlier. "Is that clear?"

23

ARAX

Z orux and Odix stare back at me in a futile display of defiance, but as I expected, their eyes drop to the floor. "Your will, Firstborn," they mutter.

I'd have preferred to avoid a scene entirely, but this can't be allowed to slide. It's not Nyx I'm worried about—he can take care of himself—it's Viola. I want to give her everything. On Zoraht, she would have been Empress. This prison planet is a poor substitute for the homeworld, but she will still be treated with the respect she deserves.

Our mate's companions wear translators. I walk over to them and introduce myself. Once the pleasantries are over, I get to the important matters. "Are you being treated well?"

They both nod. "Everyone's been really nice," Ryanna Dickson says. "Ferix even gave us his house to stay in."

"And," I hesitate before asking, "Everyone's been respectful?"

Nyx rolls his eyes at the way I tiptoe around the touchy topic. "What Arax is asking," he says bluntly, "is if anyone has tried to force themselves on you."

"They've been perfect gentlemen," Sofia Menendez

replies. "No one has even flirted with us." There's an undertone of disappointment in her voice, and as she says it, her eyes seem to linger on Rorix and Ferix.

Ah well. I might be the leader of our exile batch, but even I can't solve matters of the heart. I don't understand how the Draekon mating bond works, and I don't understand what causes us to transform when we sight our mate. It's all a mystery to me.

When the two scientists get better, I'm going to have a long conversation with them. If they intend to survive in this world, if they seek our help, then it's time for them to give up their secrets.

24

VIOLA

As soon as we're alone, the two women turn to me. "Our mate?" Sofia asks with a sly grin on her face. "Shifted to dragons?" Ryanna says at the same time. "Tell us *everything*."

We exchange stories. I tell them about being cornered by the Dwals, and how Arax and Nyx turned to dragons when they saw me, about how I was poisoned by the *kilpei* flower. "And you slept with them right after," Sofia says slowly. She gives me a troubled look. "You know it's because of the toxin, right?"

"What?"

"I spent the morning with Vulrux. This world teems with medicinal plants. The *kilpei* flower is a mild aphrodisiac."

I snort. "For the Draekon, maybe. It almost killed me."

"You probably got a higher concentration," she replies.

Her implication is clear. I wasn't in complete possession of my senses when I slept with Arax and Nyx.

And maybe I wasn't the first night, but the rest of the times I've slept with them? That was my decision. "I don't care what you think," I say firmly. "I'm attracted to Arax and Nyx. I'm not going to give them up." I don't want to get into a fight with the two women about this, and besides, we have more important things to discuss. *Like the fact that we're stuck on this world forever.*

Yikes. "Forget Arax and Nyx for a second," I begin nervously. "I don't know how to tell you this. I don't think we're going to get rescued."

They nod. "We already know," Ryanna says. "The men told us. That was a *fun* surprise. I want to punch Beirax. How dare he make this decision for us?"

Despite her words, she doesn't sound too broken-hearted at the thought of never being able to go back home. I glance at Sofia, who doesn't look upset, just resigned. "You're both taking this better than I expected," I say cautiously. "How come?"

"Maybe I'd be a lot more agitated if I had family back at home," Sofia says. "Plus, Ryanna has a theory about the Zorahn." She looks at the other woman. "Tell Viola what you told me."

"Sofia and I compared notes." Ryanna's voice is serious. "Do you realize that none of us have close family ties? That has to be part of the reason the Zorahn chose us. And after Beirax's actions, I'm not entirely convinced the trip was on the up-and-up."

"What do you mean?"

She gives me a cynical look. "I mean, that despite their pretty words and their promises of safety, personally guaranteed by the High Emperor himself, we're lab animals to the Zorahn. If we die, how much of a fuss do you think our government is going to raise? The aliens cured leukemia, Vi. The US Army is probably dying to get their hands on some alien weapon technology. They won't make a fuss about ten volunteers who signed on for fame and fortune. We're collateral damage."

"The High Emperor is Arax's brother."

Ryanna chuckles. "That makes sense," she says. "He's pretty damn bossy but really polite about it. You can tell he's used to being in charge."

"So you're okay about this? Really?"

To be honest, I think we're all in shock. When it sinks in, I'm not sure we won't be more distressed. I'm lucky; I have Arax and Nyx to comfort me. But the others?

Sofia shrugs. "I'm not thrilled about what Beirax did, but on the bright side, we survived the crash, we're alive, and we have plenty to eat and drink. We have shelter. It could be a lot worse."

"And Rorix and Ferix have nothing to do with it," Ryanna says with a sly grin.

Sofia flushes. "You're one to talk," she retorts. "You were completely checking out Thrax's ass."

Before this conversation goes high-school-hormonal, I clear my throat. "You still have to tell me what happened after we split up," I remind them.

"Let's see," Ryanna says. "When we split up, Harper was still conscious, wasn't she?"

Sofia nods. "Yes, she was. She was pretty weak on her feet, and really light-headed, but we were able to walk. We thought we were walking back to the ship."

"You got lost?"

"Horribly," Ryanna says ruefully. "We'd been walking for two hours when we reached a waterfall."

"I don't think we got very far," Sofia says. "I think we were walking in circles by that point. We were delirious with the lack of water. Harper was moving slower and slower, and she kept wanting to rest." She shudders. "It was awful."

Obviously, they didn't get eaten by the Dwals, because they're sitting in front of me. "You didn't see the big dog things?"

"Striped yellow and black, as big as a horse?" Ryanna nods. "Not at the start. We drank the water and forced Harper to stay awake long enough to drink too. Then Sofia and I tried to figure out what to do. We weren't sure how many hours of daylight we had left, and we needed to find shelter."

That must have been right around when Arax and Nyx were sucking the poison out of my body. Not that I'm going to tell the others that story. That memory is all mine.

"We thought we saw a cave behind the waterfall," Sofia says. "We were trying to figure out how to get Harper there when the damn dogs showed up." She shivers. "They started whistling to each other like they were laughing at us. You remember that scene in Jurassic Park where the raptors figure out how to open doors, and you realize the predators are a lot more intelligent that you give them credit for? That was us."

"I still had the gun you gave me," Ryanna says. "So I shot two of them."

"You did? That's *badass*."

She grins. "The guys showed up just as I was about to nail the third one. We were pretty glad to see them, I have to tell you."

Ryanna and Sofia didn't let Raiht'vi's warning spook them. They're a lot smarter than me. "They didn't shift to dragons when they saw you?"

Sofia shakes her head. "Nope. Just as well. I'm still a little shocked you aren't terrified of Arax and Nyx. Had I seen them become twenty-foot beasts, I'd still be screaming."

"I was never scared of them." I'm not sure if Sofia or

Ryanna believe me. It makes no sense that I wasn't afraid, but it's absolutely true. Even when I told myself to be wary of them, something inside me always knew I could count on Arax and Nyx.

"Well," Ryanna continues, "we gave three of them translators, and we stole Harper's to give Thrax, because, by this time, Harper was unconscious. Vulrux said we all needed to get back to the camp before the rains came."

"That's when we found out that we're stuck here," Sofia adds. "We told the men that we just needed to survive until our rescue, and Vulrux laughed bitterly and told us there was no escape."

"Because of the asteroid belt," I reply.

The three of us are alone in the dining hall. All the Draekons seem to be busy. I see them cooking, skinning furs, and chopping logs. "They're preparing for the rainy season," Sofia explains. "There's four extra mouths to feed. Possibly more, if we can find the other women."

"You know about the others?"

"Be patient," Ryanna chides. "I'm getting to that part. So, once we found out that we weren't getting rescued, we knew we had to move the others before the rains. And we had to find you, of course. We refused to go to the camp without you or the other women, but we couldn't leave Harper alone either. So we took shelter in the cave behind the falls and figured we'd come up with a plan in the morning. Ferix and Vulrux stayed with us. Thrax set out to get more Draekon to help with the injured, and Rorix went in search of you. If he couldn't track you down before the sun set, he said he'd spend the night by the spaceship, just in case you managed to find your way back."

"In the middle of the night," Sofia says, "we heard a loud roar, and we saw the flares go up. Vulrux and Ferix were freaking out about Rorix being in danger. Had it not been for us, they'd have set out to help their friend."

Yeah, that seems about right. I'm pretty sure the only reason Arax and Nyx didn't go to the ship in the middle of the night was because they had to take care of me.

"Rorix came back in the morning," Sofia continues. "He said that the women were taken by Draekon, ones he didn't recognize."

"Nyx thought they were a different exile batch," I tell them. "These guys are the fifth group that the Zorahn have exiled to this world because they tested positive for the Draekon mutation."

"Well, after that, they wouldn't listen to us anymore." Ryanna sounds quite put out by it, and I hide my grin. I get the sense that she doesn't hear the word 'no' a lot. "They insisted that they take us to camp right away for our safety. And that's pretty much it. We set out in the morning, and Thrax met us halfway there. He'd already roped in four Draekon to find you and rescue Raiht'vi and Beirax."

"That's why they didn't look too surprised to see me," I say aloud. "They already knew I existed."

We talk for another hour. The sun is starting to set again, and I can barely keep my eyes open. "I don't know about you two, but I'm wiped from the climb," I tell them. "I'm going to find Arax and Nyx and crash."

Sofia gives me a sharp look. "You climbed the cliffs?"

"Didn't you?"

They both shake their heads. "We were carried," Ryanna says. "I'd like to think I'm in good shape, but I couldn't manage that ascent. Not at the speed at which they did it."

Huh. Weird. I guess my time in the rock-climbing gym near my house finally paid off.

25

NYX

In the Lowlands, our dwellings are simple. Just a canvas of hide thrown over a simple wooden framework, thickly coated with *watlich* paste to repel the hairus.

But on the cliffs, we've allowed ourselves to get more creative. These homes don't get swept away in the floods, and we don't have to rebuild them every season.

My house is on the outskirts of the clearing. One side of it overlooks the steep cliffs, with sweeping views of the jungle. The green-and-black striped reeds of the *kunnr* trees are everywhere, with their glowing blue fruit that our mate calls vanilla pudding. Dotted here and there are the bright pink *schrit* trees, contrasting with the deeper purple hues of the *watlich*.

"This is unbelievable." Viola stands next to me and surveys the landscape. "I can't believe how beautiful it is here." She puts an arm around my waist. "You even have a porch."

The translator explains the unfamiliar word. "It's a hot world," I reply. "When we can, we want to be outside."

She shivers. "It's not that warm up here in the mountains," she replies, pulling her tattered top around her. "I have a sweater in my luggage. Pity I can't get to it."

"You have additional garments?" When the water recedes, we can make her new garments using the wool from the sturdy webs spun by the *ahuma*, but until then, I wasn't sure what we were going to do about clothing in the rainy season.

"In the hold of the spaceship," she replies, sounding resigned. "A fat lot of use it is there." She shrugs. "Ah well, such is life. Where's Arax?"

"He's checking the provisions," I reply. "Food is difficult to find in the rainy season. The *argangana* herds scatter and hide, and fruit and vegetables rot on the trees. If we don't have enough food, we'll go hungry." I smile at my mate. "We can't have that."

"When Beirax and Raiht'vi get here, there will be six new people," she says with a frown. "That's a lot of mouths to feed. Will you be able to manage?"

"We're organizing some more hunting trips," I tell her. I don't tell her that this close to the rainy season, the undertaking is fraught with peril. She'll only worry for us if she knows. "Arax will be along any moment now. Do you want to wash and rest until then?" My lips twist up in an amused smile. "Remember our promise. We intend to show you that we're not too old to pleasure you."

She flushes. "I'd love to wash," she says. "Is there another lake somewhere?"

"A lake? I think we can do better than that."

26

VIOLA

Thereʼs a bathroom.

No shower, but thereʼs a tub big enough for the Zorahn, which means itʼs more than big enough for me, and thereʼs hot water. "How?" I ask, dumbstruck. This seems like a miracle.

Nyx looks puzzled. "Where does the water come from, you mean?" he asks. "We store it during the rainy season, and we use it to bathe. For drinking, thereʼs a mountain spring not too far from here."

I guess that if you take a technologically sophisticated people and put them on an alien world for sixty years, this is what you get. Iʼm not sure that Iʼd be so industrious if the situation were flipped around. "Whatʼs the tub made of?"

"Fired clay," Nyx replies. "Thereʼs no metal in this world, so weʼve had to get creative. But we can do a lot with wood and clay."

"No kidding." I follow Nyx to another room, and lo and behold; thereʼs a huge wooden bed with a thick mattress on top of it.

I think Iʼve died and gone to heaven.

Nyx's eyes twinkle with mirth. "Did you think you'd spend the rest of your life sleeping on the mud floor of a cave, sweet one? We travel light on a hunt, but we're quite fond of our creature comforts."

Umm, yes. I sit down on the mattress, which is wonderfully soft, and sigh in pleasure. "That is exactly what I thought," I admit, chagrined. "Obviously, I was wrong."

Arax steps in just then. "The scientists are here," he says. "Vulrux is tending to them." He gives me a strangely tentative look. "Do our homes please you, *aida*?"

"Are you kidding me?" I fling my arms around his neck and kiss his lips. "This is lovely."

My conversation with Sofia and Ryanna has made me realize something. I would have slept on the floor of a cave, as long as Arax and Nyx were on either side of me. When I left Earth, I was numb with the pain of losing my father. With Arax and Nyx, I've been given a second chance, and I'm not about to squander it.

He kisses me back passionately. "The three of us will not fit in the water tub," he says, his voice regretful.

I've been climbing all day, and I must reek of sweat. "Let me bathe quickly," I whisper. "And I'll be right back."

I take the quickest bath in the history of womankind. The water is perfect, and there's a few little coarse woven washcloths stacked to the side, and a bowl of liquid with seed pods floating in it—an oily liquid Arax tells me I could use as soap. The solution has a slight herbal scent and makes me wonder what other plants might be useful to make our life easier here.

I never thought I'd use my botany skills on an alien planet.

I scrub, clean, rinse and scramble out of the tub, only to find there are no towels.

"Hey guys," I call, opening a basket to see if there's something I can at least wrap my hair in. "Do you have a towel?"

"What?" Arax says from just outside the room.

The basket is empty, so I check a shelf that holds some sweet-smelling sticks of wood—like incense. It smells a little like the smoky musk I've come to associate with my mates. "Um, a cloth or something I can use to dry off?"

Arax steps into the door holding a large cloth between his hands. "Like this?" He does a great poker face, but Nyx hovers at his back, a mischievous curl to his mouth.

"Yes... you sneaks." I wag a finger at them. "You could've left that in here with me."

"And deprive ourselves the pleasure of seeing you like this?" Arax tilts his head to the side, taking me in.

"You've seen me naked before." I tug at the towel, but he doesn't let go.

"Not like this. Lovely, shining with water, standing in my home."

His possessive growl makes my pussy quiver.

"Yeah, dripping water all over your floor." I feign irritation to cover up the way his words squeeze my heart. Sixty years he's been stuck here, away from his home. Never expecting to see a woman again, much less take a mate. "May I have the towel?"

Arax strides forward and envelops me with the cloth. "Let me, *aida*. I wish to care for you."

I bite my lip, willing myself not to cry at the way he buffs my skin, his ministrations tender and thorough. Nyx joins in, toweling off my hair with another small cloth. By the time they're done, I'm close to begging them to bend me over the tub.

I have an idea. "Arax, why don't you take a bath?"

His face goes blank. "Do I smell?"

"No, no, I just want to see you as you saw me. You know, naked and wet—"

His loincloth hits the floor.

"Like this?" He climbs in the bath. The tub is huge, but he still has to bend his legs to fit. His knees stick up out of the water, and that's not the only thing sticking up.

"Yes, exactly." I pick up the wash cloth. "I'd like to clean you."

His grin turns wicked, and I realize my mistake. Here I have seven feet of gorgeous male, skin glistening in muscled perfection, and I've offered to run my hands all over him. If I'm not careful, I'll end up a puddle on the floor.

Ho boy.

I focus hard on sluicing fresh water over him and rubbing the washcloth over the glorious contours of his chest. I do all right until I lean closer to wash his opposite shoulder, and his hands caress between my legs.

"Hey, now," I scold.

He ignores my protest. His fingers strum between my folds and convince me to widen my stance. One thick digit finds my entrance, and the washcloth falls into the water.

"Viola," Arax murmurs.

"Yes?" My hands are white-knuckled on the side of the tub, my mind on Arax's finger circling inside me.

"You dropped the cleaning cloth."

"Oh, right. Um—" His finger hooks and presses against the soft wall above my entrance. My legs tremble.

A second pair of hands clasps my hips. "I've got you." Nyx runs his hands up my sides. I'm about to thank him when something hot, hard and roughly the size of a baseball bat glides between my legs. Well, maybe not that large, but it feels huge sliding against my slick thighs.

I lean over the broad lip of the bath. My position allows

me to press my bottom into Nyx's groin and puts Arax's cock in the vicinity of my mouth. I can't resist. I close my lips around the broad, flared head.

Arax sucks in a breath, his hips jutting upward. His hands grip the sides of the tub. I hum as I tongue the underside of his cock, exploring the thick, masculine taste of him.

At my back, Nyx props me where he wants me, scooting my feet out wide. My fingers flex into a fist on Arax's taut abs as Nyx's cock probes my pussy. I'm folded over the bathtub rim, sucking as much of Arax as I can while Nyx eases deeper and deeper into me.

Arax's head drops back. Eyes closed and body taut, he slowly pumps in and out of my mouth. I wrap my left hand around the base of his cock, steadying myself with my right hand on Arax's chest. I watch his face as I swallow his rod, swirling my tongue and finding his sensitive spots.

Lost in him, I take him too deep, gag, and pull off. My teeth graze the rim of his crown. He moans, but in a good way. I do it again and curses spill from his mouth.

Fierce satisfaction shoots through me at the fact that I've made Arax completely lose control.

He strikes the side of the tub with his right hand, overcome. His body tightens, the pebbled muscles of his abs standing out in stark relief as he fights from coming too soon. I pop off and swipe my tongue lazily around his head, holding his eyes. The taste of him is addictive. He clenches his jaw, eyes blazing.

"I love the way you taste," I tell him, and he curses harshly. The translator struggles to interpret, but I don't need words to know how he's feeling.

Then Nyx sheathes his full length inside me.

"I love the way you feel," Nyx purrs, tightening his hold

on my hips as he pushes deep, his cock hitting every delicious spot inside me.

"Oh," I gasp. "Oh God." I pull my mouth off Arax's cock, clenching my eyes shut as Nyx pulls out and slams inside me again.

Arax rises out of the bath like a roused river god, water streaming off his bronzed body. He kneels in front of me, takes a fistful of my hair, and snaps his hips forward, filling my mouth with his tasty cock. I flail a moment and catch his lean hips, hanging on as one Draekon pummels my pussy, while the other owns my mouth. They glide in and out, speeding up in perfect sync.

My feet leave the floor as Nyx lifts my legs, his huge hands gripping my thighs while he powers into me.

A gentle hand catches my chin, and I meet Arax's gaze, fierce and tender and loving all at once.

"Sweet one," he whispers, and I'm overcome. I climax, careful to keep sucking his cock as my muscles quiver and my body trembles. I never thought I could fit such a big cock in my mouth, and while I can't swallow his entire length, his girth fills me perfectly. I breathe through my nose and suck as hard as I can, savoring the salty-sweet taste of him.

He pulls out and comes with a shout, tugging my hair. The sharp sensation pushes me into a series of rippling climaxes of my own.

Undeterred by my orgasm, Nyx keeps pumping into my spasming pussy. My head jerks back as he pulls my hair, tugging it like a rope until I arch my back. His thrusts slow to a hard, rhythmic pounding that sends waves of pleasure spiraling through me again.

Arax captures my mouth, tugging on my nipples. I lose my grip on the tub, but the large Draekon catches my shoulders and holds me still as Nyx finishes with a roar.

When the men lift me, I'm helpless and weak as a babe. My pussy is sore, and I have red marks on my stomach from the side of the tub. They towel me off carefully and lay me on the bed, curling up on either side of me.

Nyx palms the back of my neck, pulling me close for a moment. He kisses me softly, holding my eyes. "I love you, *aida*. You are the fire in my heart."

"The fire in my soul," Arax murmurs, running a finger down my cheek until I turn to him. He presses his lips against mine. "One that will never die." It sounds like a promise.

Both men capture my hands and press my palm to their chests, over their hearts. Their gaze is so intent and penetrating, for a moment I have a hard time meeting their eyes.

Wow. It got really serious in here for a moment. I almost say that out loud, but for a change, I gulp down all the dumb jokes that come to mind.

"Thanks, guys," I say weakly.

After a moment, I draw my hands back. They release me, but we can't undo the moment.

I swallow hard and try to process the way I'm feeling. I'd never had a guy tell me... much less two guys at the same time.

But that isn't why I'm freaking out. Do they mean it when they say they love me? The sex was mind-blowing, as always, but they still haven't been able to transform.

What if I'm not really their mate? What if they transform to dragons when they see one of the other women? What if it's Olivia, or May or Paige or Felicity or Bryce that is their real mate?

Jealousy makes my stomach lurch. I reach out and grab their arms, and the touch of their skin reassures me.

"Viola?" Arax's voice is thick with concern. "What's wrong?"

I shake my head. "Just... felt a little shaky."

Arax frowns as if he knows I'm lying.

Nyx strokes my back. "You've had a long journey," he says soothingly. "Everything in your life has changed. I remember the first days after we were exiled. It took some time for us to accept it."

"It's not that," I say. I don't want to keep lying to them. "I'm sorry... it's just a lot to take in."

"Take as long as you need, *aida*. There is no hurry."

I cast about for a new topic of discussion. "I really like your house. Why don't you live here year round?"

"All the food is in the lowlands," Arax replies. His lips quirk as if he knows I'm changing the subject, but he allows it. "The climb takes too long for us to do it daily. It's just easier to live down there in the dry season."

"If you were Draekons, you could fly up and down."

"True." Nyx lies on his back, looking up at the ceiling. "It'll be easier to carry our stores up too."

I nod as if I'm thinking about this, but I can't get my mind off their earlier words. *I love you. You are the fire in my heart.*

"Can I ask you something?" I whisper. "Are you sure I'm your mate? Because we've slept together a lot of times, and you still haven't transformed."

"Viola, don't worry." Arax's voice is soothing. "You are of a different species. The mating bond will take time, but it will happen." He takes my hand and places it on his chest. "I know you are our mate, as does the beast inside me."

I really hope he's right.

27

ARAX

The next week is a blur as we scramble to accommodate the extra mouths we have to feed. We hunt. We fish. We forage far and wide for leafy greens, scaly vegetables, and delicate food. Our mate likes *kunnr*, so I make sure we gather as many of the glowing blue fruit as we can carry.

Then there is the problem of the badly wounded scientists. Vulrux decides he needs a medicinal herb to treat them that only grows in the lowlands. I send Zorux and Odix to look for it, which has the added advantage of getting the two traditionalists out of camp.

We wait for the rains. Every night, Uzzan is shrouded in the sky, but though the air is thick and heavy with moisture, the deluge does not come.

As the days go by, the mad rush dies down. The medicinal herbs work their magic, and Beirax's wounds begin to knit. Raiht'vi has suffered a concussion, but after a week of forced rest, she too seems to heal.

Five human women are still missing, but unfortunately, there's nothing that we can do about them right now. If our theory is right, then there is another exile camp somewhere west of the Na'Lung Cliffs, west of where the spaceship crashed, but we can't go looking for it. Between the Na'Lung Cliffs and the next set of mountains is a twelve-day journey. We can't risk being trapped in the lowlands for such a long time, not when the rains are imminent.

Though the preparation for the rainy season takes up much of my time, I spend as many hours as I can with our mate. Her body is changing. Her muscles are leaner, and her skin glows with health. She has more stamina, and she climbs the cliffs with ease.

She still hasn't realized that the changes in her body are brought on by the Draekon mutation, and truth be told, I'm afraid to tell her. On Earth as well as in Zoraht, men and women choose their partners. I'm not sure how Viola would react when she hears that her body is being adapted to bear Draekon youngling, but I suspect it won't be with happiness.

Though it is shameful behavior, I hide the truth from her, hoping she'll realize it for herself.

I'VE JUST RETURNED from a hunt when Vulrux sends word that he wants to see me. "Beirax is finally healthy enough to be questioned," he says. "Do you want to talk to him?"

Talk to him? *I want to hurt the scientist.* Yes, it was his actions that brought Viola Lewis to me, but I'm fully aware that it wasn't my mate's choice to be exiled on this world. Beirax is injured, and we will feed him until he's well. After that, he'll be put on trial. He's directly responsible for the death of Mannix and Janet Cane. He will not escape justice.

Vulrux leads me into Beirax's room and leaves us alone. The scientist is propped up against the walls and appears to be half-dozing. When I enter, his eyes flutter open.

"I'm Arax, leader of this exile batch." I give the scientist a cold glare. It doesn't make me feel good to yell at a man who's obviously wounded, but what Beirax did is beyond forgiveness.

"I know who you are, Arax, Firstborn of Zoraht," he responds. "I know all fourteen of you. There were ten Draekons in the first exile batch, the ones sent to this planet seven hundred and fifty years ago, and I know their names. I've read the secret sections of the ThoughtVaults, the ones accessible only to the High Emperor, the Head of the Council and the Firstborn. More than that, I've found the hidden records, the ones not in the ThoughtVaults, the ones that tell the truth of the Draekon race." He gives me a challenging look. "Knowledge is power, Firstborn of Zoraht, and I'm the only person in this world who knows the full truth."

His lips twist in a cynical smile. "I've heard it spoken that you've found your mate, but you haven't shifted since. Would you like to know why?"

I'm not a fool. Beirax wants to trade his secrets for a pardon, but I'm not in a forgiving mood. "No," I say flatly. "I know enough of my history. When scientists meddle, people die." I take a deep breath and try to calm the fire within. "Make no mistake, Beirax. You will stand trial for your crimes."

I'm sitting outside Nyx's house with a cup of kunnr wine, staring into the distance, when Nyx finds me. The two of us have been away from camp on two different hunting trips, and I haven't seen him for the last three days. "There you are," he says when he catches sight of me. "I've been looking all over for you."

I raise an eyebrow. "What's the matter?"

"I think we should go to the spaceship," he says. "Viola said she had some belongings in the hold, but she couldn't get it open." He sits down next to me. "Our mate is happy," he says carefully. "But I also think she's a little homesick. We should get her possessions before they're ruined in the rainfall."

"She's homesick?" I ask, concerned. I can't change the way she's feeling, but our mate shouldn't be alone when she's in pain. We should be with her. "Where is she now?"

"She climbed down to the lake with the other two human women," he replies. "Ferix and Rorix went with them."

I think rapidly. The sun is starting to sink in the sky, but if we leave now, we can make it to the cave where we first made love to Viola before it gets too dark. The spaceship is a four-hour journey. If we leave at dawn tomorrow, we'll be able to retrieve Viola's possessions and return by nightfall.

"We have to make haste," Nyx says. "If the rains come..."

If the rains come, our lives are at risk. On the prison planet, the rains aren't a gentle mist, the way they were in Giflan. Here, the skies open, and the water pours down, and the rivers overflow their banks in the blink of an eye. We have to hurry if we want to be there and back before the deluge.

But if the contents of the spaceship's hold will make our mate happy, then we will get them for her. It's that simple.

"Let's go."

"We should tell Viola where we are going," Nyx says. "She will be concerned if we are missing."

"We'll probably run into her on the way down." I see Vulrux hurrying to the house where the Earth woman, Harper Boyd, rests. She's still in a coma, and Vulrux seems unsure what to do to revive her. The Earth healer, Sofia

Menendez, doesn't seem to know what to do either. "But just in case we don't, I'll tell Vulrux where we're going, and he'll pass on the message to Viola."

Vulrux is my cousin. His mother was my father's sister, and the two of us grew up together. I trust him with my life.

Nyx nods agreement. A flash of lightning pierces the sky, and a worried expression crosses his face. "If we're going, we need to go right now, Arax."

We follow Vulrux into the house where the two scientists are recovering, and we find him examining Raiht'vi. I fill him in on our plan. His lips tighten in disapproval, but he doesn't protest. "Don't linger," is all he says. "Are you taking anyone else with you?"

"No." I can't ask one of my companions to take this risk. "It'll just be Nyx and I. Don't tell Viola why we've gone; I want it to be a surprise. I don't want her to worry, though. Tell her we'll be back in no time."

28

VIOLA

Sofia and Ryanna want to go swimming in the lake. They insist I come with them, and since Arax and Nyx are away on hunts, I agree.

My mood is dark. It's been almost ten days since Arax, Nyx, and I first made love, but guess what? No dragons.

And it's freaking me out.

I'm distracted the entire time we're away. Rorix and Ferix shamelessly show off their swimming prowess, while Sofia and Ryanna giggle and egg them on, but even their antics can't cheer me up.

Back at camp, Vulrux tells me that Arax and Nyx are off on yet another hunt. "I thought we had plenty of food?" I question sharply.

Vulrux shrugs philosophically. "You know what a worrier my cousin is," he says. "He likes to be prepared."

"How very Boy Scout of him," I reply acidly. Immediately, I feel bad about snapping at Arax's cousin. The tall, calm healer is one of my favorite people in the camp. "Sorry, Vulrux. I'm in a bad mood, that's all. Please forgive me."

He waves away my apology with an easy smile. "It is of

no concern, Viola Lewis. I'm about to check in on Harper
Boyd before I turn in for the night. Would you like to walk
with me?"

"No." A sudden thought crosses my mind. I've been
trying to figure out why Arax and Nyx haven't transformed,
but I've been looking in the wrong places.

It was Beirax who brought us to this planet, specifically
so we could mate with the Draekons. It is Beirax who wants
the Draekons restored to their former glory. Surely then,
Beirax would know why Arax and Nyx aren't becoming
dragons.

Vulrux shares Arax's viewpoint that the scientist is
responsible for Janet and Mannix's deaths; he won't approve
of me talking to Beirax. I wait until he's out of sight before
making my way rapidly to the house where the two Zorahn
patients are recuperating.

I have to know the truth.

No one is around when I slip into Beirax's room. He
seems to be asleep, but as soon as I enter, he opens his eyes.
The Zorahn must sleep like a cat. "I have some questions for
you," I say bluntly, skipping the pleasantries.

"Of course you do. You're wondering why your so-called
mates haven't taken their dragon forms." His lips twist into a
smile that doesn't reach his eyes. "You're the talk of the
entire exile batch, Viola Lewis. I admit, I thought you'd seek
me out sooner."

"Well?" I demand tautly. "Why haven't they transformed? What do you know?"

He struggles to sit up, and I'm angry enough that I don't
help. Some of Arax's high-handedness must be rubbing off
on me. "We chose the Earth women with the best likelihood
of compatibility," he says finally.

A cold ball of dread knots in my heart. "What do you mean by that?"

"The mysterious illness that's sweeping Zoraht, what did you think that was?" He sneers at me. "An outbreak of the mutation. In the past, the Draekon mutation manifested in only one in a million births, but something changed, because during the last Testing, we didn't find ten or even twenty Zorahn that tested positive. *We found two thousand.*"

"You exiled two thousand people?" I ask him, shocked. Tearing ten or twenty people from their homes and loved ones is bad, but two thousand?

His lips tighten, and he refuses to answer. I switch tacks. "What does that have to do with Earth?"

"Stupid human. Isn't it obvious? A thousand years ago, we used genetic matter from Zoraht and from Earth to create the Draekons. Where else would we go to destroy them?"

I frown at Beirax. "I heard you on the ship. You don't want to destroy the Draekon. You said you wanted to restore them to glory."

Beirax nods. "There is much infighting in the Council of Scientists, but we are clear on one thing. We will not allow the High Emperor to destroy our greatest creation."

His eyes gleam with the madness of a true fanatic. "Lenox hopes to find something in your genes to eradicate the Draekon mutation," he says. "But the Order of the Crimson Flame has a different goal. We will bring the Draekon back, and with them as our loyal soldiers, we will rise to power."

He gives me an indifferent look. "Arax and Nyx have transformed once. Other mates will be found if you aren't adequate."

That hard lump of dread in my heart grows larger. We're

all lab animals to Beirax. Arax, Nyx, me. We are just one big science experiment. "You're talking about Sofia and Ryanna?" I ask, my voice cold. "What makes you think they'll do any better than me?"

He bares his teeth at me in a humorless smile. "You must think we're fools, Viola Lewis. We have more power than you think. Do you think this is our only attempt? We will try and try again until we succeed. The Order of the Crimson Flame will prevail."

The scientist is insane. I pivot on my heels and stalk out of the room. I need to find Arax and Nyx and tell them what I've learned.

I'M ALMOST outside the house when I hear someone call my name. It's Raiht'vi. "Viola Lewis," she addresses me, a strange light in her eyes, "Are the rumors true? You have mated with the Draekons?"

Jeez. Nice to know that my sex life is a topic of conversation for the entire planet. "Why do you want to know?" I demand.

"You must not complete the bond," she insists. Her voice is weak, and when she holds her hand out in my direction, there's a distinct tremble in it, but the conviction in her tone startles me. "Beirax did not share all the facts with you. Why do you think the Draekons were exterminated in the first place? Because when they transformed into dragons, they lost the ability to tell friend from foe."

Her eyes bore into mine. "If they turn, they will kill us all. If I were you," she says with calm, terrifying intensity, "I would kill myself before the mating bond is complete. I would do it to protect my people."

"No." I shake my head violently. Raiht'vi is wrong. She

thought the Draekons would tear her to pieces, and instead, Vulrux is tending to her wounds. She thought Arax and Nyx were dangerous beasts, and instead, they've sheltered her as she's recuperated. "I've had enough of your lies, your half-truths, your refusal to take responsibility for the actions of the scientists. You're wrong. I *know* Arax and Nyx. *They would never harm any of us.* They don't even care that they haven't transformed after our mating."

"Is that so?" Her tone is as contemptuous as Beirax's was. "If that's true, then why have your mates set off in search of the Draekons that took the Earth women? They hunger for the transformation, Viola Lewis. Perhaps they hope that the other Draekons may be able to guide them. Or perhaps they seek a different mate." Her face twists into a sneer, and her words knife into my gut. "A better one."

I stare at her, my thoughts jumbled in my brain. Arax and Nyx couldn't have gone in search of the other Draekons. So many times, I've heard them explain that the journey is dangerous this close to the rainy season. I *know* they don't care enough about the transformation to risk their lives, and despite Raiht'vi's poisonous words, I *know* they wouldn't cheat on me.

Then it dawns on me. I'm the one who's freaking out that they haven't become dragons.

They're not doing it for them. They're doing it for me.

I have to find them and tell them that I love them, and that's the only thing that matters. *Before it's too late.*

29

VIOLA

Even I'm not stupid enough to take on the *hairus*, so I wait until daybreak. As soon as the sun rises, I set out. All I have with me is a pack with some food and water in it. I've thought about taking Beirax's gun, but it's still with Ryanna, and if my friend finds out what I intend to do, I'm sure she'll stop me.

This is a stupid idea, Vi.

I know, I know. Arax and Nyx can take care of themselves much better than I can. I'm positive that they won't put themselves in danger with reckless abandon. Especially Arax. But I still feel responsible. How many times have I worried about their inability to transform into Draekons? *A lot.* I can't help thinking that this is my fault.

I hurry down the cliff face with daredevil speed. My father would be proud of his little goat. He was afraid of heights, and he was always very impressed whenever he saw me climb.

I make excellent time getting to the lowlands. When we climbed up, it took us almost an entire day to make it to the top, but judging from the position of the sun, I've descended a lot faster than that. If I had to guess, it's noon, which means I've made the trip in six hours.

Of course, it's easier going down than climbing up.

Once I get to the bottom of the Na'Lung cliffs, I drink some water and set off in the direction of the spaceship. If Arax and Nyx were going to look for the other Draekon, the trail would begin there.

Unfortunately, I've been walking for about an hour and a half when I realize I'm completely lost. I'm in a section of the lowlands that I don't remember seeing, thick with the pink *schrit* trees, their bark covered with the orange fungus responsible for Harper's coma.

"I'm pretty sure I didn't come this way before," I say out loud, looking around at the dense jungle that surrounds me. Is this the same set of *schrit* trees that Harper brushed against? I don't think so. If it were the same set of trees, I should have passed the river on my journey, and I haven't.

Don't panic, Vi. All I need to do is keep calm, retrace my steps back to the Na'Lung cliffs, and start over. I have food and water. *There's no need to freak out.*

Umm, the Dwals? A much more sensible voice inside me prods. *Remember them?*

Yeah. I should have taken Ryanna's gun, or asked one of the Draekon to go with me. Vulrux wouldn't have approved of my recklessness, but he wouldn't have let me go alone. Right now, I'd even be glad to have gloomy and grouchy Haldax watching my back.

My heart hammers in my chest as I turn around and go back the way I came. As I walk, I talk to myself. Hey, there's no one else around, no one to think I'm a lunatic. "This isn't your brightest idea, Vi," I say. "Yes, you want to find Arax and Nyx, but shouldn't you have thought this through?"

Yes, inner-voice-Viola says at once.

"Well, I had to," I argue, though I'm aware that I'm arguing with myself. "It's a twelve-day journey to the other mountain range. It's about to rain. I have to stop Arax and Nyx before they do something really stupid."

Inner-Viola isn't done pointing out the holes in my plan. *Perhaps you should have sent someone who has a better sense of direction than you,* she says snidely.

I'm about to concede the point when I see a familiar-looking section of the lowlands. If I'm not mistaken, this is the turnoff for the river. Here, ten days ago, Arax and Nyx morphed into the Draekon and rescued me from three Dwals.

Are you sure, Vi?

I can't risk getting lost again. Already, I'm hours behind Arax and Nyx, and the more I delay, the less chance I have of catching up with them. My half-baked plan definitely didn't include time for walking around in circles.

There's only one thing to do, and that's to head to the river. I'm reasonably certain that if I see the spot where the Dwals almost ate me, I'd recognize it.

Nyx's voice sounds in my head. *The Dwals lurk near the water, looking for easy prey.*

Okay, fine. I need a weapon. I break a branch off a nearby tree and fortified by the thick staff, I head toward the river.

I tell myself I'm not nervous, *and I almost believe it.*

30

VIOLA

Two Draekons are waiting at the water edge.

As soon as I round the corner and see them, I freeze in my tracks. I haven't seen these Draekons before, I'm convinced of it. I've met the fourteen exiles that live in Arax's camp.

These men are strangers from a different exile batch. Their hair is long and matted. They're completely naked, and their skin is coated with a white mud. The only thing they wear is a pouch of some kind, slung across their hips.

They look primitive. Barbaric.

My heart hammers in my chest, so loud that I'm afraid that they'll hear me. I grip the stick in my hand so tightly that my knuckles turn white. I can't hope to outrun them. My only option is to pray that they haven't seen me.

It's too late. Their nostrils flare, as if they can track my scent. Their heads swivel in my direction, and in the blink of an eye, they bound toward me, wild, exultant expressions on their faces.

It takes all the courage I have to stand still, but I force

myself to stay where I am. I can't look afraid. Who knows what might happen if they sense fear?

"Who is this?" The Draekon who addresses me has dirty-blond hair and piercing green eyes. "Could this be another human female?"

"Translating Old Zor to English," my translator intones. "Unknown dialect. Estimated translation accuracy: sixty-five percent."

Unknown dialect. These Draekons have been on the prison planet so long that their language has evolved beyond the translator's ability.

A cold fear trickles down my spine. "Who are you?" I force the words out through dry lips. "Were you exiled from Zoraht? When?"

They give me blank looks of incomprehension. My gaze flies to their ears, and my heart sinks. No translator. They're not going to be able to understand a word I say.

The other Draekon reaches out and touches my hair, his expression awestruck. "Liorax and Zunix have found a human mate," he says. He lifts a strand to his nose and breathes deeply. My insides churn. "Are you human, little one?"

The Draekons smell me and touch me, their movements more animal than human. I'm very, *very* afraid. At any moment, the situation could escalate to violence. These men are a lot more primitive than Arax's exile batch. What if they take me by force? What if they've raped the other girls?

That thought makes my pulse race with terror. "Did you take Olivia, Paige, Felicity, Bryce, and May?" I demand. My palms are damp with sweat, and I'm positive they can smell my nerves, but I won't scream. I won't show them how terrified I am. "Are they alive? Are they safe? What have you done with them?"

They ignore me.

The blond Draekon frowns. "She is afraid." His voice turns soothing, as if he's addressing a spooked pet, and he strokes my arm. "Do not be afraid of us, little human," he croons. "We mean you no harm."

"She is not our mate," the other man says. "We do not transform for her."

"No. But there are others in camp, and we will take her to them."

I shrink back in horror. "Please no," I beg them. "I already have mates. Please let me go."

Their eyes fill with concern and they lift their hands in the air. "We will care for you, little human," one of them says, his voice gentle. "Do not worry. You have nothing to fear."

"I smell her terror, Cax. She doesn't seem to want to come with us."

No shit, Sherlock.

The blond man frowns. "We can't leave her here," he replies. "The beasts will tear her from limb to limb. The rains threaten. We must take her to safety." He puts his big hands around my waist and unceremoniously tosses me over his shoulder. My stick falls to the ground.

I scream in rage and fear. They can't take me away; I won't let them. I beat the Draekon's back, my hands clenched into fists, but the man doesn't even seem to register my blows.

I'm in big, big trouble. My throat tightens as I imagine Arax and Nyx searching for me, wondering where I went. They won't be able to track me when the rains come. I might never see them again.

No. I won't let that happen. I have to fight back.

"Help," I yell at the top of my voice, even though I'm on a

sparsely-inhabited alien planet and no one can hear me. "Help me."

ARAX

The moment we hear Viola's scream, my heart stops.

We drop the packs we carry and begin to run. *Our mate is in danger.*

Time slows down.

The first transformation was excruciating. *Not this time.* As I run, the dragon emerges from within me. There isn't any pain. My skin stretches, and my muscles expand. My claws lengthen. Wings erupt from my back.

This time, the trapped creature doesn't revel in its freedom. *Protect our mate,* it says fiercely. *She is all that matters.*

My wings unfurl. I roar with anger at the thought of someone hurting our mate. Jumping into the air, I take flight, Nyx at my side.

VIOLA

"Fuck, fuck, fuck," I chant, as the Draekons prepare to take me away.

Then I hear loud, booming roars of anger, and two dark shapes blot out the light from the sky.

The instant the Draekons holding me catch sight of the threat, they swear loudly. Dropping me, they flee through the brush. In the blink of an eye, they are out of sight, lost in the jungle.

Two dragons land on the bank of the river. The air shimmies around them as they morph back to men. It's Arax and Nyx. My mates.

I run to them, tears streaming down my cheeks. Throwing my arms around them, I cling to them, seeking comfort in their strong arms. "They were going to take me," I say through my sobs. "I thought I'd never see you again."

"Who?" Arax asks sharply. "What happened?"

Nyx's fingers gently wipe the teardrops away. "Viola," he says softly, stroking my back. "You're safe. We're here. We will die before we let anything happen to you."

"There were two Draekons here," I tell them, my voice trembling. "They were going to take me to their camp." I take a deep breath. "They knew I was human. They probably took the others." *Oh God oh God oh God.* "We have to find them."

Nyx kneels at the spot where the two men plunged through the forest. "They haven't made an effort to conceal their trail," he says. "We can follow them."

Before either of us can reply, multiple flashes of lightning illuminate the sky, followed almost immediately by an ominous roll of thunder.

"No." Arax shakes his head. "The rains are almost here. We can't risk it. We need to protect Viola."

He gives me a reassuring look. "Climb on Nyx's back when we transform," he orders calmly. "We will make it to the Na'Lung Cliffs unharmed, sweet one. You have nothing to worry about."

Right. Silly me. I must be in shock from my near-abduction, because it has *just* occurred to me that Arax and Nyx transformed into dragons to save me. And now they can change at will? It's pretty damn convenient timing.

Dragons can fly. I'm going to ride through the air on the back of a dragon. I wanted adventure? I'm getting it.

They both back away from me and start to change. The air around us grows colder, and when I exhale, I can see my breath. Frost coats the tips of nearby leaves, and the section of the river closest to me ices over.

If I see it a million times, I don't think I'll have words to describe the transformation. One moment, they're men, and then, in a flash, two massive dragons hulk in front of me.

Sofia asked me if I was terrified when they became dragons, and I told her I wasn't. I'm not lying. I know fear. When the two strange Draekons came for me, I was petrified. But I've never been afraid of Nyx and Arax. They might be dragons, but they are my mates, and I know that they will protect me with their lives.

Also, the whole 'morphing into a fearsome predator' thing? Totally hot. Call me superficial, but I'm the mate of the biggest, baddest Draekons, and I like it.

Arax's crimson tail lashes the ground, bringing me back to the urgency of the situation. I force myself to stop ogling them, and I crawl up Nyx's tail. *It's like riding a horse, Vi,* I tell myself. *A really large horse with wings and scales. You can do this. Legs astride the neck, and hang on tight.*

Okay, I might be a little nervous. When Nyx launches into the air, I gasp, and when the skies open and rain pummels down on us, I scream loudly.

Then Arax flies above me, positioning himself so his body blocks out the bulk of the rain. Nyx swoops down to grab something in the jungle, and then, we fly home.

BACK AT CAMP, I pace back and forth. Though I've wrapped a towel around my body, I'm still shivering. "You should have seen them," I say, my voice shrill with panic. "They didn't even wear clothes. They were primitive. Barbaric." The other exile batch must have been on the prison planet so long that the trappings of civilization have been stripped away. "What if they hurt the other women?"

Arax folds me into his arms. "Viola," he says, his voice calm. "Breathe, sweet one." He exchanges a glance at Nyx. "The previous exile batch was sent a year before us. How could they have diminished so quickly?"

"Maybe they didn't have the Firstborn of Zoraht bossing them around," Nyx suggests mildly. He laces his fingers in mine. "We can't find them in the rain, *aida*," he says quietly. "Even in dragon form, our eyes cannot see in the downpour. The water washes away their scents. You know that."

"I do." I try to dismiss the hard knot of fear in my chest.

Arax crouches next to me and looks into my eyes. "Viola, I promise you. As soon as the deluge ends, we will look for them. You have my word."

Their concern is a warm blanket of comfort. I hold on to my mates, and I cling to hope. The Draekons from the other tribe were primitive, but they had recognized my terror. They had assured me I had nothing to fear from them. I can only hope they show Olivia, May, Bryce, Felicity and Paige the same care.

"Until then," Arax continues, "I don't think we should tell the others about your encounter. The Earth women seem in good spirits at the moment, but I fear they are in shock. At some point, it will sink in that they're stuck on this planet for the rest of their lives." He brushes his lips over mine. "You need to be strong, *aida*. Your companions will look to you for solace."

Sixty years ago, Arax acted as a leader. Now, he's telling me I need to do the same thing.

He's right. I need to stay calm, and I need to lead by example. I take a deep, steadying breath and nod in agreement.

"Which brings me to my next question." Arax's expression turns grim. "What you were doing in the lowlands alone?"

Ah, hell.

I was hoping they'd forget to ask me that question, but

judging from Arax's stony look, I'm in trouble. I should back down, but I'm too stubborn. "Are you yelling at me?" I ask him, lifting my chin and glaring at my two infuriating Draekons. "I know you were trying to find the exile batch. You even got Vulrux to lie for you. I had to try and stop you, you stupid lugs. I didn't want you to drown in the rains."

Nyx runs his hand through his hair. "What are you talking about, *aida*?" he asks, his expression filled with confusion. "We weren't trying to find the exile batch. We went to the spaceship."

"But Raiht'vi said that you set off to find the other Draekon."

Arax shakes his head. "The other Draekon? We told Vulrux we were going to the ship. Raiht'vi was half-asleep. Maybe she was confused?"

I look from Arax to Nyx. Arax's expression is turning dark, and I know that if I continue this conversation, Raiht'vi is in for some serious trouble from my Draekon mates. I'm not sure the Zorahn scientist doesn't deserve to be punished. I can't help but remember her words. *If I were you, I would kill myself before the mating bond is complete. I would do it to protect my people.*

Yet I hold my tongue. I don't trust either Zorahn scientist, but if Arax banishes them, I won't be able to find out what their true motives are. And my instincts tell me it's important that I understand what's going on. There are wheels within wheels here, and both Raiht'vi and Beirax are involved. I'm sure of it.

"Maybe," I concede.

AN HOUR LATER, I've had a bath. I'm warm and dry, lying naked on the bed, my mates on either side of me.

"Explain the morphing. Why couldn't you change before, and what happened?"

Outside, visibility has been reduced almost to nothing. The rain beats down, as thick as a wall, and from the safety of the cliff-top camp, I can see animals flee to higher ground. I have no doubt that if I were stuck in the lowlands, I'd drown.

Arax's fingers stroke my hair. "Remember, the Zorahn scientists are geneticists," he says. "When we mated for the first time, our fluids mingled. Your body started a process of transformation."

Of course. When he points it out, I realize that the clues have been there from the start. My increased stamina. My newfound muscles. Even my vastly improved ability to climb and run. Before I slept with Arax and Nyx, I couldn't keep up with them; they had to carry me on their backs. After the bonding, however, I matched them step for step.

I have no idea why it took me so long to see what's been staring me in the face. If my Ph.D. adviser were here, she'd be terribly disappointed in me.

"It wasn't just your body that was changing. Ours were too. The process took a few days." Arax shrugs like it's no big deal. "But once it was complete, we were able to transform."

Hmm. I put my long-forgotten scientist hat on. "I'm assuming my body is changing so I become ready to bear Draekon babies?"

Arax's gaze rests on me. "Does that worry you?"

Strangely, no. The idea of creating a little Draekon baby, one with a piece of Arax, Nyx, and me in it, is tantalizing. "No," I confess. "I think I'd like that."

Arax and Nyx hug me tight. They'll probably deny it if I ask them, but I'm pretty sure I can see a sheen of tears in both men's eyes, and I can understand their emotions.

They've been exiled for sixty years, cut off from family, from women, from any semblance of love. To be honest, I'm a little weepy at the idea of giving them a baby.

"I love you," I whisper. The second I say those words, a feeling of rightness sweeps over me. It's true. If you'd told me two weeks ago that I'd fall in love with two aliens who can morph into dragons, I'd have laughed my head off. I'd have replied that I was done with love; my father's death caused too much damage, and my heart was forever frozen.

Then I met Arax and Nyx, and I discovered how wrong I was. I'm in love with them, not because I'm their mate, and not because they can change into dragons. I'm in love with them because they care for me. Right from the start, they've protected me, and they've been at my side, ready to caress me and comfort me. They've made what should be a difficult situation so much better.

Arax and Nyx smile back at me. "We love you too, Viola Lewis," Arax says solemnly.

Nyx nods agreement. A wide grin breaks out on his face. "We have something for you," he says, jumping out of bed and hurrying out of the room. I just have time to give Arax a confused look—what's Nyx talking about?—before the dark-haired Draekon comes back into the room, holding a suitcase in his hands. "I thought you might want your belongings," he says. "That's why we went to the spaceship. We had to open the hold and retrieve your possessions before the rainfall."

I stare at my bright pink luggage, my throat thick with tears. They did this for me. Just so I'd be happy.

I throw my arms around them, pulling the two men close and hugging them tight. Then I shift my attention to their cocks. After all, I need to thank them for my luggage.

And I know a really good way to do it.

"Come here, gentlemen." I scoot back on the bed, and they follow eagerly.

Nyx grins at me. "You want us to prove to you we aren't too old to please our mate?"

"Um, no. You proved that more than enough times in the past few days. I'll never look at a bath the same way again."

Arax approaches, his movements silky and cat-like. He's hunting me, I realize, just as Nyx pounces in a sneak attack.

I laugh wildly, pretending to fight him off. He catches my hands with ridiculous ease, and holds them with one of his, freeing his left hand to cup my breast.

I sigh and arch my back, pushing into his palm.

"How is it you guys have been here for sixty years, and you know just how to touch a woman?"

"Not just any woman," Arax says. "You. Our mate."

"We are very good hunters." Nyx's fingers prove his words, sliding straight to the target, hooking around the entrance of my pussy to my soft, welcoming core. He pulls in a "come hither" motion, and little sparks of pleasure rain through me, lighting fires wherever they land.

I roll into him, pressing my face into the curve of his neck to muffle my gasps.

He pulls my leg over his hip and slides inside me. I'm more than ready for him. Behind me, Arax stretches my bottom hole with his fingers, his thick precum both soothing the burn and warming me for his cock.

I sigh with pleasure as their cocks replace their fingers.

Even on their sides, my mates thrust with gentle power. They tease my nipples and tug at strands of my hair, and I'm driven wild with raw desire.

We climax together, our bodies twined so closely I don't know where I end and they begin.

"My heart," Arax tells me fiercely.

"My soul," Nyx presses my hand to his chest.

"My mates." I blink back tears. It only took a trip through space and surviving a coup, a crash, poison fruit, a kidnap attempt and alien predators, but I've found my soul-mates—both of them.

EPILOGUE
VULRUX

Arax believes that he and Nyx are the first to transform into Draekon in a thousand years.

He's wrong.

Deep in the underground laboratories of the Crimson Citadel, a splinter group of scientists conducts their experiments on the Draekon, trying to understand why the mating bond causes the morphing.

Sixty years ago, I was drawn there one night by a tugging in my soul, by a need that twisted my insides with urgency. *Go quick,* a creature within me seemed to whisper. *They need you.*

What I found? Two people, strapped on tables, held down by thick leather straps that ran across their body. The man was bleeding from a thousand cuts, his bright blue blood seeping into the wood below.

When I laid eyes on them, something happened. The air thickened. Time came to a stop. In my mind's eye, I saw threads linking the three of us.

Then I transformed.

. . .

I KNOW Arax and Nyx aren't the first Draekons to change to dragons in a thousand years. That day in the Citadel, my soul recognized my mate, and when I saw her, the transformation took place. I became Draekon, as did the male prisoner.

But in the Crimson Citadel, the scientists reign supreme. As soon as I morphed, alarms sounded. Guards appeared out of nowhere, armed with weapons that couldn't pierce my skin.

They didn't aim their weapons at me.

No. The scientists of Zoraht are many things, but they are never stupid. They didn't try to subdue me.

They did the only thing they could. They killed the woman. Our mate.

In shock, in despair and in grief, I became a man again. I didn't fight back—what was the point? She was dead. My soul withered, and everything came to an end.

FOR SIXTY YEARS, I've kept my transformation a secret, but I don't think I can keep the truth concealed any longer.

Because when the Earth women appear in our camp and I see the unconscious woman in their midst, the golden threads weave once more, binding Dennox and me to her.

Against all odds, we've been given another chance. Another mate. An Earth woman who has brushed against the most poisonous fungus on this world, a woman who might never emerge from her coma.

Harper Boyd is our mate.

THANK you for reading Draekon Mate!

The prison planet adventures continue in Draekon Fire. This time, it's Harper's turn to find her mates. Keep reading for a preview, or click here to purchase it.

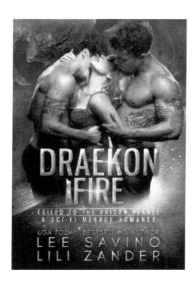

Crazy jungle planet. Killer orange fungus. Crimson snakes in the water. The worst part? While I was in a coma, I seem to have acquired two dragon mates.

When I wake from my coma, the first thing I see are two hot aliens.

And I'm informed that they're my mates.

I don't think so.

This isn't the story of Sleeping Beauty, and the two sexy, possessive, Draekons aren't my fairy tale princes.

I'm certainly not going to wake up, kiss them, and live

happily ever after on this stupid prison planet, where everything's out to kill me.

Not happening.

Not even if they heal me from my injuries and nurse me back to health.

Not even if they protect me, care me, and keep me safe.

Not even if their abs could grace the cover of every men's fitness magazine back home.

Sleeping Beauty isn't going to kiss her Draekons. She's going to find a way back home.

Draekon Fire is the second book in the Dragons in Exile series. It's a full-length, standalone science fiction dragon-shifter MFM menage romance story featuring a snarky human female, and two sexy aliens that are determined to claim their mate. (No M/M) Happily-ever-after guaranteed!

One-click DRAEKON FIRE now

OR

Get **DRAEKON DESIRE** and binge-read the entire **DRAGONS IN EXILE** series in one heavily discounted, 1000+ page boxed set!

Are you all caught up with the Draekons? Don't miss any of the books.

DRAGONS IN EXILE

DRAEKON DESIRE - Binge-read the entire **DRAGONS IN EXILE** series in one heavily discounted, 1000+ page boxed set!

Draekon Mate - Viola's story
Draekon Fire - Harper's story
Draekon Heart - Ryanna's story
Draekon Abduction - Olivia's story
Draekon Destiny - Felicity's story
Daughter of Draekons - Harper's birth story
Draekon Fever - Sofia's story
Draekon Rogue - Bryce's story
Draekon Holiday - A holiday story

❧

REBEL FORCE
Draekon Warrior - Alice & Kadir
Draekon Conquerer - Lani & Ruhan
Draekon Pirate - Diana & Mirak
Draekon Warlord - Naomi & Danek
Draekon Guardian - Liz & Sixth - coming soon!

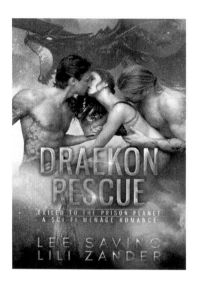

*The **Must Love Draekons** newsletter is your source for all things Draekon. Subscribe today and receive a free copy of Draekon Rescue, a special Draekon story not available for sale.*

A PREVIEW OF DRAEKON FIRE

CHAPTER 1

Dennox:

Once again, I watch my mate die in front of my eyes, and once again, I'm helpless to act.

A dozen people are clustered around Harper Boyd's bedside. The human woman has been in a coma for twelve moons. She breathes on her own, and when we hold water to her lips, she drinks. But she hasn't eaten in twelve days. Her body wastes away to nothing in front of our eyes, and there is nothing any of us can do to stop it.

"I'm completely out of ideas," the human healer, Sofia Menendez says, a frustrated look on her face. "Viola, any thoughts?"

Viola Lewis, the human mate of Arax and Nyx, shakes her head helplessly. "I've got nothing." She turns to Vulrux. "Tell us again what happened to Rorix. How did he come out of his coma?"

"The situations are nothing alike." I speak for the first

time, my voice harsh. The Firstborn looks up, surprise on his face at my interruption. Too late, I realize that no-one knows why I'm drawn to this human woman's bedside. No-one knows that Harper Boyd is my mate.

Except for Vulrux, Thirdborn of Zoraht. My pair-bond feels the same complex set of emotions that I do. Vulrux is a healer who couldn't save his mate. I'm a soldier who couldn't protect her. Our shame is etched deep into our souls, and we've never spoken of the events that led to our exile.

"Rorix was in a waking trance," I continue. "He didn't speak, and he didn't appear to recognize us, but he still ate and drank." I take a deep breath. "This human woman is frail. She isn't Draekon. She doesn't have long to live."

Viola Lewis has a stricken expression on her face at my words. Ryanna Dickson, a dark-haired human woman, straightens, her eyes flashing with anger. "Harper isn't frail," she says tightly. "She's not helpless, and neither are we. If there is a way to save her, we will find it."

Nyx puts his arm around his mate and gives me an annoyed look. "Even the thieves on the streets of Vissa learn tact," he bites out. "It's a pity that the Zoraken aren't taught manners."

No. We're taught instead to kill.

I stare back at Nyx, refusing to back down. The thief has never lost a mate. Who is he to speak to me of tact? Has he lived through the pain of watching two mates die? Has he ever felt as helpless as I do at this moment? I am cursed by the lives I've taken, and the fabric of my soul lies in shreds. That must be why the fates taunt me so.

"Enough." Vulrux steps between the two of us, his voice calm. "Our arguments do not help Harper Boyd."

He's right. Unfortunately, we're out of ideas. Vulrux has

tried every medicinal herb in his stores on the human woman. Sofia Menendez has given her drugs from her meager supplies. Nothing has revived our mate.

Slowly, the others trickle away. I stay where I am, ignoring Arax's thoughtful stare. When I'm alone with Harper Boyd, I lay my hand over hers. The woman's flesh is hot to the touch, her skin the color of an angry sea. The toxin lingers in her blood, but unlike the mild venom of the *kilpei* plant, it can't be sucked out.

When Vulrux had carried her up the cliffs on his back, unwilling to entrust the precious human to any of the others, our mate had been wearing the strange clothing of her people, a dark blue garment that clung to her body, highlighting every curve. Now, she's got a towel draped over her, the thin silvery fabric made from the sturdy webs spun by the *ahuma*, and nothing else. The dragon inside me purrs at the thought of her nakedness and demands I complete the mating bond, but I am Zoraken, and I have honor. This woman is more than a soft body. She is a person with thoughts and wishes of her own, and whatever her dreams of her future were, I'm sure they didn't involve being stranded on an alien planet and dying from a poisonous fungus.

"Harper Boyd," I say softly. "I was a soldier of the Empire. I killed in the name of the High Emperor, and though the mind-wipes prevent me from remembering everything, I know that my soul is stained and tattered." I take a deep breath. "The Zoraken do not take mates. We do not have families. We die in battle, and I have no cause to expect more."

Yet I do.

She stirs in her sleep, and I tense, hoping against hope that she will wake. Vulrux must sense her movement because he reappears at her bedside. His shoulders slump when he realizes that she's still unconscious. "Nothing?" he asks me.

I shake my head.

"The first time," he says quietly, "I was young. I had lost before I knew what loss was. This time—" His voice trails off.

I seldom let my thoughts wander to the time I was held captive by the scientists. There was a woman there, but the dragon within me hadn't recognized her as my mate. Not until Vulrux had shown up to complete the triad.

It was the same way when Vulrux had set this human woman down on his bed. The instant the three of us were in the same room, the golden bonds had brightened, but they'd faded almost immediately.

Harper Boyd is dying.

"You are both fools." A harsh voice interrupts us. I look up to see one of the scientists in the doorway. *Raiht'vi.*

Every time I look at the white-clad woman, animosity rises in my blood. I've searched my memories—those still left to me after repeated mind-wipes—and I can't recollect her. Then again, the images in my mind are fragmented, a result of the cocktail of drugs that have been forced into me from the time I was conscripted.

"What do you mean?" Vulrux's voice is mild, but I sense the tautly stretched anger underneath.

"You think with your hearts," she snaps, moving into the room. Her steps are slow, and her face contorts in pain as she moves. She is still healing from her wounds, but that doesn't stop her from glaring at us. "Try using your minds instead."

"You speak in riddles," I say icily. "Explain."

"Before the Zoraken, there were the Draekons," she

replies. "They were the perfect soldier race. They were made to be invulnerable." She stares at me with a strange expression on her face. "You are Draekon, soldier. The poisons on this world cannot harm you. Pass that immunity on to your mate."

Our heads snap up in shock at her words. "How do you know that Harper Boyd is our mate?" Vulrux asks, his hands clenching into fists. "No one else knows."

"Many have eyes and do not see."

I am a soldier of the Empire. I know how to *persuade* Raiht'vi to part with her secrets, but I doubt that the First-born will give us permission to torture the scientist. Besides, even though her words are riddled with mystery, she's telling us something important. "What immunity? We cannot resist the fungus any more than the humans can. Rorix was in a coma for six months."

She huffs impatiently. "The Draekons adapt. If Rorix were to brush against the same fungus today, it would give him nothing other than a rash. His immunity will have passed onto you."

My spine prickles with unease. "I don't trust you. I will not risk hurting our mate."

"Her words make sense." The human healer, Sofia Menendez stands in the doorway. I wonder how long she's been there. In normal times, I would have heard her approach before she got near, but I'm distracted by the lovely golden-haired woman next to me, her breathing labored as she struggles to live. "In essence, that's how vaccines work on Earth. I think we should try it."

"No." Vulrux's lips tighten. "I agree with Dennox. My experience tells me that scientists are not to be trusted."

Raiht'vi moves swiftly. Before I can react, she grabs Vulrux's knife from his belt and slices a deep cut in Harper

Boyd's palm. Sofia shrieks as red blood gushes out from the wound. "Are you insane?" the human healer says angrily. "What have you done?"

Raiht'vi faces her squarely. "The human doesn't have time for your endless debates," she snarls. She turns to the two of us. "Act now to save your mate, Draekon. Let your blood mingle with hers."

My jaw tightens. "If this fails," I promise the crimson-haired scientist, "I will see you dead of my own hands."

She doesn't reply. She grabs the human healer by the hand, and half-drags, half-pushes her from the room. With sick fear in my heart, I pull my knife out and slice a cut in my palm. Vulrux does the same. The two of us take Harper's hand in ours. Our bright blue blood mingles with her rich red.

We wait. The moments tick by. Harper Boyd's breathing stutters and seems to cease, and time comes to a halt. I'm ready to find the scientist, wrap my hands around her throat and squeeze when Vulrux's voice stops me. "Wait."

Golden threads appear in my mind's eye, chains that bind Vulrux and me to the woman on the bed. As we hold her hand, the bonds strengthen. The deep blue poison in Harper Boyd's blood recedes, and her skin regains a pinkish hue. Her eyelashes flutter.

The beast within me exults. *Our mate lives,* it growls in triumph. *As soon as she wakes, we will claim her.*

But the beast doesn't rule me. The man does. And the man has learned that the mate-bond brings only pain.

CHAPTER 2

Harper:

When I open my eyes, several realizations sweep over me, each one more disconcerting than the next.

I have no idea where I am.

Two hot, naked-to-the-waist guys are in the room with me. They're holding my hand in theirs, and as I watch, drops of blue blood spill on the silver sheet.

And I'm not wearing a stitch of clothing.

I'm not sure if I should freak out or part my legs for the hunks.

I settle for neither. Drama isn't really my style, and though I have nothing against hook-up culture, if I'm going to put out, I'd like a meal and some attempt at conversation first. In a world where courtship has been replaced by swipe-rights, that makes me high-maintenance.

Hang on, Harper. Two strange guys are holding your hand, their blood is freaking blue, and you're thinking about Tinder?

The memories slowly start to return. Alien spaceship. Crash landing. Injured Zorahns leaking blue blood. Green and blue moons, pink skies.

Viola, Ryanna, Sofia, and I had set out to find food and water so we could survive the next week until the Zorahns used their superior technology and rescued us. We were walking toward Penis Mountain, but I'd tripped, and some orange goo had tried to kill me.

Since I'm not dead, I guess I've been rescued and treated, and unless blue blood is super-common in the galaxy, the two men at my side must be Zorahn.

I look around covertly. I thought Zoraht would be filled with sleek metal and glass towers and little airships buzzing about in the sky. *Probably because I read too much science-*

fiction as a kid. This room isn't very high-tech. The texture of the walls looks like wood, though the colors—pink, green, and black—remind me that I'm not on Earth. The effect is a little psychedelic. *Groovy, baby.*

The two Zorahn aren't looking at my face; their attention is focused on my arm. I'm assuming they're observing the effects of the orange jello from hell. Their expressions are somber. I swallow nervously. "Is it bad?"

Both their heads snap up at the sound of my voice. The taller and broader of the two men says something, relief etched on his face.

Unfortunately for me, I have no idea what his words mean.

Great. I've managed to lose my translator.

"Hey, buddy?" I try to sit up, and my head swims. I feel nauseous. Ugh. I hate being sick. "You know one of those golden thingies that go in my ear and shock the heck out of me? I'm missing mine. You can't rustle up a spare, can you?"

I point to my right ear at the same time. I'm being a little flippant since I assume neither man can understand me, but at my snark, both men's eyebrows rise, and an amused smile curls around the lips of the non-linebacker. He gets to his feet and moves to a corner, returning a minute later with my own personal babel-fish.

Shit. I see the golden translator embedded in his ear, and it dawns on me. I can't understand them, but they can understand me just fine, and they probably think I'm an idiot.

My cheeks heat as I reach for the little device. Non-linebacker, who has dark hair that falls in sexy, shaggy waves around his face, and vividly green eyes, doesn't hand it to me. Instead, his fingers stroke my forehead and he tucks a strand of hair behind my ears, before inserting the golden disk into my right ear.

Whoa. Tingles. Tingles everywhere as the hot alien touches me. My arm might be sore, and there appears to be a gash in my palm, but my girl-bits are humming happy songs.

Stupid girl bits. I've met Beirax, and the tall alien has a massive stick up his butt. Zorahn men might be easy on the eye—and trust me, these two are very easy on my baby blues—but fun to hang out with they're not.

I sit up, slower this time. "Where am I?" I ask them. "Is this Zoraht? Where are the others? Are they safe?"

Mr. Linebacker speaks for the first time. "Your companions are well, Harper Boyd." When he smiles at me, his caramel eyes warm and kind, my insides do a funny flip. I thought Beirax was huge, but this Zorahn makes Beirax seem puny. He's tall, broad and muscled. His chest is criss-crossed with scars, but they don't do anything to detract from his gorgeousness. If anything, they just make him hotter.

"Where's Viola?" She'd told Sofia and Ryanna to take me back to the ship, while she went to find water and food. The two women were supposed to put me back into stasis. Is that what happened? "Is she okay? Did you find her before you whisked us off the prison planet?"

An expression of consternation flashes over the linebacker's face. He looks at the other alien, who clears his throat. "This might come as a shock," he says gently. "You aren't on Zoraht. You're still on the prison planet."

My brain struggles to comprehend his words. "But why?" I stammer. "The spaceship went down. They'd have to know we crashed—they must have radar, or whatever they use in space. Why haven't they come for us? They told us we were under the personal protection of the High Emperor. Surely that's got to be good for a rescue mission."

The green-eyed alien raises an eyebrow. "Lenox's word?" His tone makes it clear he doesn't think much of the High Emperor. That's not a good sign. The other Zorahn seemed to think that Lenox was the best thing that had happened since sliced bread.

Another thought occurs to me, one that causes anxiety to rise in my chest. What had Viola said before we set out? This was the world in which the Zorahn exiled their criminals. Draekon, she'd called them.

The two aliens sitting next to me aren't Zorahn doctors. They're not to be trusted. They're to be feared.

My arm throbs and my head spins. The room goes blurry, and I fall into a dead faint.

Click here to keep reading Draekon Fire, book 2 of the *Dragons in Exile* series. The book is a standalone MFM menage romance with a guaranteed HEA!

OR

Get **DRAEKON DESIRE** and binge-read the entire **DRAGONS IN EXILE** series in one heavily discounted, 1000+ page boxed set!

ABOUT THE AUTHORS

Lili Zander is the sci-fi romance loving alter-ego of Tara Crescent. She lives in Toronto. She enjoys reading sci-fi and fantasy, and thinks a great romance makes every book better.

Find Lili at:
www.lilizander.com
www.facebook.com/authorlilizander
Email her at lili@lilizander.com

Lee Savino is a USA today bestselling author. She's also a mom and a choco-holic. She's written a bunch of books—all of them are "smexy" romance. Smexy, as in "smart and sexy."

Download a free book from www.leesavino.com.

Find Lee at:
www.leesavino.com
www.facebook.com/leesavinoauthor

BOOKS BY LILI ZANDER

The Vampires' Blood Mate (A Reverse Harem Paranormal Romance)

Night of the Shayde

Blood of the Shayde

Soul of the Shayde

or read the complete trilogy in one boxed set...

The Vampires' Blood Mate

Blood Prophecy (A Dragon Shifter Reverse Harem Romance)

Dragon's Thief

Dragon's Curse

Dragon's Hope

Dragon's Ruin

Dragon's Treasure

or

Dragon's Fire (the omnibus edition, containing all the Blood Prophecy episodes) *and a bonus story,* Dragon's Ghost.

Suzie and the Alien

BOOKS BY LEE SAVINO

Hey there. It's me, Lee Savino, your fearless author of smexy, smexy romance (smart + sexy). I'm glad you read this book. If you're like me, you're wondering what to read next. Let me help you out...

If you haven't visited my website...seriously, go sign up for the free Berserker book. It puts you on my awesome sauce email list and I send out stuff all the time via email that you can't get anywhere else. ;) leesavino.com

Then check out...

My **Berserker series:** These huge, dominant shifter warriors will stop at nothing to claim the women who can free them from the Berserker curse These books are based on an Old Norse poem I studied in college, but writing heroines who find freedom in their sexual desires is my therapy after years of religious repression. They're...ahem...quite kinky, so stay away if you don't want a fair bit of BDSM.

The series is broken into two, all set in the same world and time period:

The Berserker Saga
Berserker Brides

Then I have a few series with cowriters! Yay!

The Draekon series with Lili Zander
The Tsenturion Masters with Golden Angel
The Bad Boy Alpha series with Renee Rose

Contemporary Romance. Check out Her Marine Daddy-free on all sites except Amazon (until they decide to make it free for me). More contemporary romance books coming soon!

Manufactured by Amazon.ca
Bolton, ON

39996279R00118